Dana slid into the seat next to Kent. She didn't want to think about what had stirred her to make that move.

"Look at me." No matter the cause, the effect landed her next to his warm body. "Please?" She'd beg if she had to.

Right now, here under the glaring bright lights, on a rumbling train, she wanted more than a taste of a wild ride.

Kent turned his handsome face toward her. It was all she needed. Taking a deep breath, she mounted his lap. Her hands anchored his face. She gazed into those beautiful eyes.

"Kiss me?" Her question hung softly in the air, begging for his assent.

His gaze shifted to her mouth. Under her fingers, she felt his chin lift towards her face.

The kiss, the first contact, was soft, tentative, an introduction of sorts to each other's lips. She wrenched her mouth away because logic wanted a point of intrusion. Her breathing was heavy, as if she'd hit the treadmill for a challenging mile on an incline.

Books by Michelle Monkou

Harlequin Kimani Arabesque

Sweet Surrender
Here and Now
Straight to the Heart
No One But You
Gamble on Love
Only in Paradise
Trail of Kisses
The Millionaire's Ultimate Catch
If I Had You
Racing Hearts
Passionate Game
One of a Kind

Kimani Press Arabesque

Open Your Heart
Finders Keepers
Give Love
Making Promises
Island Rendezvous

MICHELLE MONKOU

became a world traveler at the age of three, when she left her birthplace of London, England, and moved to Guyana, South America. She then moved to the United States as a young teen.

Michelle was nominated for the 2003 Emma Award for Favorite New Author, and continues to write romances with complex characters and intricate plots. Visit her website for further information, at www.michellemonkou.com, or contact her at michellemonkou@comcast.net.

One
OF A
KIND

MICHELLE MONKOU

HARLEQUIN® KIMANI™ ROMANCE

Francis Ray, an extraordinary colleague, friend, and author, will be missed. Thanks, Francis, for your pioneering footsteps that opened doors, created paths, and gifted a wonderful legacy with your stories.

ISBN-13: 978-0-373-86344-0

ONE OF A KIND

Copyright © 2014 by Michelle Monkou

For questions and comments about the quality of this book please contact us at CustomerService@Harlequin.com.

HARLEQUIN®
www.Harlequin.com

Printed in U.S.A.

Dear Reader,

It's me again, celebrating the first book in my new family series. The Meadows will welcome all of you into the fold with the advisory to enter at your own risk—LOL. I loved TV dramas like *Falcon Crest* and *Dallas,* which had strong matriarchs who ruled the roost. No matter how crazy the family became, they never forgot that blood was thicker than water.

One of a Kind opens the curtain on the Meadows family. Grace Meadows stands proud and strong as the domineering grandmother with a hidden softness toward her grandchildren. Could it be that the iron lady is a romantic at heart? I hope you laugh, are poignantly moved and fall in love with Kent and Dana.

Raise your favorite romantic beverage to the Meadows family.

Peace,

Michelle

My new series is centered around Grace Meadows, bigger than life, complicated, inspiring, a smidgen of the fantastic person who is my mother, Doreen.

Chapter 1

Kent Fraser pulled up in front of his parents' home in Islington, a borough of London, and parked. Family dinner was a twice-a-month event when he and his stepbrother and stepsister headed back to their home base. No matter where they were, short of living overseas, they stuck to the tradition. If he bothered to be honest, they stuck to the tradition because he insisted. Dinners, reunions, BBQs helped him stay connected with the blended family and not be the graft that needed to be sawed away. His mother had a new husband and two new children from his previous marriage. She'd moved on with life and with love.

Kent, on the other hand, erected a solid wall around his heart to ward off the expected complications that came with family life. He had to move on, but his heels were firmly dug in to hinder any forward movement. Life promised to be much simpler when he threw himself into his career. Love, well, that was like relying on a leaking cup to quench one's thirst—unreliable and inadequate.

Camille, his mother, and stepfather, Alister, wanted him to feel as though he belonged. And he really did want to fit in.

Over ten years had passed since his mother's divorce from his father had split apart not only money and emotions, but had also shattered lives. The breakdown in their marriage had started much earlier, as they had been a mismatched pair. Surviving the side effects was difficult and ongoing. His father hadn't bothered to stay in touch, disappearing like a vapor trail after the divorce proceedings were finalized.

"Kent, you're on time." His mom leaned in for the customary kiss on her cheek. She took the wine he offered and headed into the kitchen.

"Kent, good to see you." Alister shook his hand and moved in for an awkward hug.

"You, too."

"Laci and Ben are in the sitting room," his mother shouted from the kitchen, amidst the ringing sounds of pots being moved from one place to the other.

Kent entered the room and immediately hugged his step-siblings until they laughingly protested.

"You all look so tanned." Both of their sandy brown heads had lightened into a halo of golden-brown curls.

Laci grinned. "We were in Costa del Sol, Spain. Duh. Thanks for the suggestion, by the way. The driving service you'd contacted met us at the airport and whisked us away for the best holiday experience."

"Next time, I'm bringing some friends, so I can act posh with them." Ben had too much of a gentle, amiable soul to be considered snobbish. However, he attended a private secondary school where most of the students were born with titles of nobility and an air of entitlement.

"Stop spoiling them," his mother chided him. She ushered in a teasing scent of dinner in her wake.

"Stop spoiling us." His stepfather's smile barely shifted his lips. The attempt resulted in a tight-faced grimace.

"I don't mind." Kent spoke slowly to reiterate his point.

His mother sent him a silent plea from behind her spectacles. *No skirmishes tonight.* Concern knitted her brow. Once again, his gifts appeared to do the opposite of what he'd aimed.

Like buying his mother this house.

What else should he have done when earning millions as an executive leadership coach? His three-year-old company and personal services drew solicitations from top companies from just about every industry.

Because of the years Kent had spent with his mum and even at the beginning of his career, scraping by at poverty level, he had developed a conservative streak. He hoarded his earnings in various funds and invested steadily in technology businesses, beverage companies, and a bit in the financial services sector. At the same time, he had a desire to spend and shower his mother with her heart's desires. This had nothing to do with Alister's ability to provide for his new family. Kent had made a personal vow when his father left that she'd never have to rely on another man for her well-being.

One Fraser had been a flaming disaster when it came to providing for his wife and son. Kent planned to stick to the promise he had made his mother out of honor and love for her. He wanted to redeem the name.

During the next hour, the mood around dinner came and went with the usual dry politeness. His parents talked about the changes to the neighborhood and the new taxes implemented on driving into the city. Then it petered out on guessing if and when the British royal couple, newly parents, would have a large family.

Laci and Ben soothed the undercurrent of tension with eager questions about where they could go skiing, never mentioning the obvious, that it was at Kent's expense. Soon they were fantasizing about the Swiss Alps and jet setting with celebrities on the slopes. Kent appreciated their enthusiasm. That's how his gifts should be appreciated, instead of his mother's and stepfather's tentative restraint. The teenagers peppered him with enough travel suggestions that he realized planning their Christmas holiday would be fun and over-the-top decadent, just because he could.

After dinner, there wasn't much point in hanging around. And yet, he did not want to head back to his empty flat in Kensington. However, his fans, Laci and Ben, took their leave to head home to their mother, who shared custody. They had classes the next day.

Now, he was left with his mom and stepfather to painfully generate conversation around general, safe subjects like weather, the economy and football—as long as he didn't go against Chelsea. Before he left, he wanted to share his good news.

Kent began the careful steering. "The business is going well." A bit of a thorny subject among them.

"Yes, dear?" His mother cleared the dishes, shooing off his offers of help.

"I may have to add two more to the staff."

"That's good, dear." Camille's voice was muffled by the water filling the sink.

Kent waited until the water stopped. "I'm glad that I took the plunge and opened up my own business. It was most certainly a risk." A risk that he had never regretted after working for ten years in sales and marketing firms, even during university.

"Made no sense to leave a solid career. Times are hard, these days. Lots of people need jobs." Alister opened the newspaper, effectively hiding his face, although his judgment spoke volumes.

"Had to do it. No time is ever perfect." How could he convince a man who was pushing fifteen to twenty years at the same job? A man who didn't like his daily routine interrupted, especially by Kent's drive-by visits with gifts. "I did research before I opened the business."

"Still, could have been a disaster," Alister replied in a flat monotone. He snapped the newspaper.

Kent turned his attention to his mother who was now rinsing off the dishes. "I might be going to America." He waited for a joyful exclamation.

"That's nice, dear."

"What on earth for?" Alister lowered the newspaper enough for his curiosity to show in his eyes and wrinkled brow.

"Got a call from Meadows Media."

"Never heard of it." The newspaper moved back into its original position.

"You've never heard of Grace Meadows? She's major. She's…"

"Maybe in the U.S., dear. Never heard of her." Camille paused in her task and stuck her head out of the kitchen.

"She owns several companies. She's written books. A lot of women look up to her because she built this business and still worked while being a wife and mother." Kent recited as many facts as he could from memory about Grace Meadows, hoping that would impress his mother and Alister.

His mother stepped back into the room. "Nothing wrong with being a housewife."

Oh, great. He'd managed to offend his mother.

"It's 'homemaker,' honey." The newspaper lowered. "See, I do know what's happening outside my mundane life."

Kent decided to leave the semantics alone and push through the quicksand. "Grace Meadows is interested in hiring me to coach their next CEO and president."

"That's nice, dear." Camille sat at the table next to Kent with a calm, small smile. "Don't work yourself to death. Come up for air." Her advice accompanied a soft pat on his hand.

"What's the point of having a coach? At that point in your career, you should know what you're doing. It's not a football game, for heaven's sake." Done with the newspaper, Alister snapped it closed and tossed it on a pile of other papers.

"Do you think that you'd like to visit America?" Kent hoped his mom would say yes. He remembered all the postcards that his father would send from various parts of the world. They were all lies, but the pictures had stuck in Kent's mind along with his other goal—that he would travel the world someday.

"Good heavens, why?" His mother switched her loyalty, going from patting his hand to taking her husband's. "I'm comfortable right here. We had the royal wedding, the Queen's Jubilee, and the Olympics. People need to come to England, not the other way around."

The fact that his stepfather had never flown wasn't mentioned. Alister always sabotaged any holiday plans to go beyond the comforts of a train or travel by car.

Kent continued with his good news. "It's not final yet. The details are being ironed out. But this job would be different since I tend to work with smaller companies and lesser-known CEOs." And why in the world had he been so lucky to be solicited—by Grace Meadows? A chance meeting had placed him on her radar.

"So, share. What do *they* do?"

Kent wanted to hug his mother for always trying to create a peaceful bridge between Alister and him.

"They have a small cable company, magazines and radio, and probably more businesses than I'm aware of."

"Can you figure out what the word is for five across?" His mother passed the crossword puzzle in the newspaper over to her husband.

They huddled over the black-and-white squares, pondering possible answers. Kent sighed. Pushing a boulder uphill had to be easier than this.

At thirty years old, he shouldn't need his parents' approval, and he shouldn't want it. He was supposedly on top of the world, as one magazine had described him. Another publication had spotlighted him, attaching silly labels like "one of the gods of Olympus" because of his talent, looks and his height of six-and-a-half feet. If he truly lived up to the Olympus hype, why should he care what mere mortals thought of him and his accomplishments?

Because deep down, opinions did matter. If he pursued something, he wanted it to be a success and was willing to put in the labor and time to make it happen.

A kiss for his mum and a handshake for Alister served as farewell parting. Another dinner was tucked away in the family memories. His next career move shared with no hurrah.

Kent drove off, heading into the city. He didn't want to go home. No one was there—that was the way he wanted it. Except, lately, a weird vibe would sneak in and hit him in some unknown space between his head and heart. He couldn't make that statement with as much bravado as was expected of an avowed and eligible bachelor.

Clear success was only in one part of his life—his career. Whenever he talked about his business and his accomplishments, the hurt from his father's betrayal leaked from its hiding place. He had something to prove.

Kent had no desire to return to his earlier life as a poor boy in public housing. Any pangs to resolve his single state had to take a backseat. With the potential of a new project, his motivation was high to refocus on his future—the executive coaching business. He wanted to scale higher walls, set records, move mountains and even those pesky boulders.

Filling his mind with work blanketed over the void of not having a special woman in his life. Observing his mother and stepfather enjoy their home life, though, had created a subtle shift, increasing the longing within him to be a husband and partner. To have a best friend in the woman who would spend her life with him. What he wanted and the reality of such happiness seemed miles apart. Since his quest to find a special woman wasn't happening anytime soon, he'd latch on to work and its rigorous demands.

Kent pulled up at his favorite pub. The late-drinking crowd could be heard from the edges of the parking lot. The boisterous din would help to alleviate his melancholy. The doors swung open, burping up a few of the pub's patrons. Kent slipped in and was immediately sucked into the warm, boozy climate. He ordered a Guinness and looked around for any of his usual crew.

"Kent, over here."

The remarkable, booming voice could belong to none other than his college flatmate. Kent sidled his way through the crowd.

"Conrad, fancy seeing you here. Your second home." Kent laughed. "What's been happening with you?" He practically screamed each word over the din, relying on his friend's ability to lip-read.

"Just made redundant."

"Bloody hell." No wonder Conrad was in the pub, although, as memory served, he always knew where the thriving pubs were located in any city. "Economy is still a pisser."

"An understatement." Conrad drained his glass and waved his hand to get the waitress's attention.

"Where are you living these days? Nearby?"

"For the moment. Should get evicted from my girl's place as soon as she finds out. The witch only wanted me because I'd pay the rent for services rendered." Conrad winked.

"You do know that's not called a girlfriend."

His friend laughed hard. But over the next hour, it didn't take long for the downer effects of alcohol to hit. His joviality diminished. "What's the point of having a business degree if there are no businesses?"

"It's all about the experience." Kent had the same business degree as Conrad, but he had been lucky to get apprenticeships with great companies and mentors who had reached out and pulled him along. By the time he'd graduated and landed his first job as a company's comptroller, he had managed to jump over many of the potholes to climb the corporate ladder. Then he had moved to operations and administration, ending in sales and marketing.

In his last year at that company, he worked two jobs, as a trainer for the corporation's sales force, and also as an online university teacher of lower-level marketing courses. Then, a very satisfied business owner had translated his appreciation for Kent's sales-staff training into a low-interest loan to start a coaching business.

"I was in bloody ridiculous marketing. The part of the

company that gets cut and outsourced in a heartbeat." Conrad took a long swig of his fresh mug of Guinness. "Maybe life is telling me to make a change. I should be overjoyed that an opportunity has been shoved up my—"

Kent put a firm hold on Conrad's drinking hand and pulled it back down to the table. Time to pull the cover over the drinking well for the night. Instead of seeking a female's company, Kent was now offering rehabilitative services for his recently unemployed, heavily alcohol-sedated college friend.

Kent managed to get Conrad into his car and hoped his friend would not share his stomach contents with him. Now he really was heading for home to his flat in Kensington. Thankfully it wasn't far away. By the time he got there, Conrad was even more out of it, but managed to hurl his stomach contents onto the sidewalk, as soon as they exited the car. Slowly and with much exertion, Kent hoisted his friend into his house and onto the closest sofa. There was no way that they would make it upstairs. He pulled off Conrad's shoes, adjusted his legs and placed a sofa cushion under his head.

"And here I thought that I was competing with a young tart for your attention," a familiar female voice remarked.

Kent twisted around, startled by his visitor.

Agatha, Kent's girlfriend—and recently turned ex—stood on the stairs in sexy, very revealing lingerie. The silk robe she wore hung open, revealing one long slender leg. She didn't seem to care that he did have a visitor. She sashayed her way over to the drunken heap in the living room.

"Is that Conrad?" She tilted Conrad's face toward her with two fingers, as if he was dirty to the touch.

Kent nodded. "Our long-lost friend with unfortunate luck."

"Looks like he's not going anywhere." She looked bored with Conrad and edged closer to Kent. Before he could move, she slipped her hand over his backside and squeezed. "And I'm not going anywhere, either."

The see-through lingerie revealing her naked, luscious form should have been enough to make Kent hard. Her hand, still caressing his butt, should have stirred his longing to be in her. As he looked at her, trying to grasp what he'd seen in her beyond good, healthy sexual appetite, he could latch onto nothing. His desire had evaporated a long time ago. But that didn't stop her theatrics, including her descent down the stairs like a starlet, like a siren trying to seduce him, like someone who couldn't take no for an answer.

He sidestepped out of her hand's reach. Without a word, Kent continued tending to Conrad, heading off to retrieve a blanket.

"Tired?" Agatha wasn't giving up.

Kent didn't respond, tossing the cover over Conrad's snoring form.

"I could massage your back."

Kent sighed. He hated to be rude, but he would have to throw her out. He was tired and wanted to get in his bed. Alone.

"You're tap-dancing." Agatha smirked. She fluffed out her hair. The motion allowed the soft, clinging fabric to outline her naked body.

"Doing my best Billy Elliot impression as we speak." Kent averted his eyes.

Agatha wrapped the panels of the robe around her body. She stared at Conrad, but Kent knew that she wasn't really looking at his incapacitated friend. She nodded, as if she had engaged in a conversation with an unknown person and come to a decision. She headed up the stairs.

"I'll get my stuff."

He nodded. Waiting. He listened to her move around the second floor. She stomped between the bedroom and bathroom. Finally, she came down dressed in a blouse and pants, her heels clicking against the wood treads of the stairs. An oversized bag hung over her shoulder. The smoldering expression was now replaced with hostility.

"I'll need the key." Kent didn't like loose ends, and he didn't like when a hint wasn't taken. Granted, his breakups weren't reality TV–worthy. But he had made it clear that their brief fling had ended and expected that she would demonstrate her acceptance by handing back his key.

"I guess we've moved from needing time to think to jumping off this bloody ride."

The problem was, Kent didn't know what he wanted. As he felt Agatha's hurt and anger, he knew, and he'd always known, that she wasn't The One. Agatha wanted him to take a break to rethink their situation. That meant holding on for no good reason. She was right—it was time for her to jump off.

"Wherever you've retreated to in your mind, I know it's a solo trip. But I stupidly thought you'd remember that I was here, in the flesh, and have always been here."

"I never made promises." Kent wasn't in the mood for a breakup fight. That had already happened a week ago.

"That's right. You have a ridiculous aversion to commitment."

"And you want to change the rules that you were fine with in the beginning."

"That's what lovers do. Are you capable of loving, Kent?" Her voice's tremor was more about rage than grief. Another tidbit he'd learned during their fling.

Kent remained silent.

"I don't think that you've faced the truth that you can't

love. Can't ever be vulnerable." Her eyes glistened with tears, but there was no mistaking their frosty glare. "Truth hurts, doesn't it?"

Kent could have stopped this train wreck with a few apologetic words and a lustful glance. Tonight could have been like their other nights: eat dinner with his family, come home, get snogged and wake up to a brand-new day. Even now, as Agatha railed, he could put out a detour sign and find his way back to where they had started. But his voice remained muted. His hands remained tucked in his trouser pockets. His heart remained off-limits.

Agatha opened her purse and took out the key. "Here. It's been an interesting six months in your world."

Kent didn't know whether to respond with gratitude or continued silence. In the end, he reached out and took the key. He could tell from her pained expression that she'd hoped there would be a last-minute reprieve, a cease-fire.

Now, he did move and opened the door. He'd had breakups before, some messier than others. This was quiet, refined, but still heart-wrenching, for her, he'd imagine. He leaned in to give her a peck on the cheek, one that he hoped let her know that he wished her well and hoped for good things and good boyfriends to come her way.

Instead, Agatha maintained her dignity by avoiding his lips, and went out into the night. He waited until she got in her car and pulled off, before stepping in and closing the door.

Kent normally did the pursuing and managed the relationships he was in, keeping them all brief. Kind words and regret were all he could offer. No way was he ever going to follow in his father's footsteps, to repeatedly offer his heart to every woman who bothered to pay him attention. The price of being too quick to fall in love was steep.

Years ago, when his parents were still married, an angry

husband came to the house with his children in tow to tell Kent's father what he thought of him, except his father wasn't home. Instead, the sordid details of an affair were revealed to his mum. Kent had stayed in his bedroom, listening to the pain that betrayal caused. His mum somehow could heal and believe again. For Kent, he preferred to stay in a separate bubble with the belief that relationships were like a minefield. Unless he was careful every step of the way, a careless foot was bound to set off a calamity. He'd never regretted his decisions to end a relationship. But he didn't relish rehashing them, either.

He sighed. What else could go wrong?

The sound of Conrad coughing and then throwing up in his sitting room made him wish that he hadn't asked the question.

Kent looked up at nothing in particular. "Please, can I get a sign that my life isn't heading for the toilet!"

His phone chirped with an incoming email from his assistant. It read: Meadows Media has accepted the contract bid. Please call at your earliest convenience.

Chapter 2

"Wake up, sleepyhead."

Dana brushed away the offending hand that latched onto her shoulder. The familiar voice of its owner was more irritating than frightening.

"You've got to get up. Your grandmother is on the warpath."

Her grandmother, Grace Meadows, always had a startling effect on the nervous system when she harbored a bad mood, a semipermanent condition.

With that piece of intel, Dana was wide awake. Yet, she still rebelled by keeping her eyes shut.

"Stop goofing. You shouldn't make it worse."

"Or what? She's going to spank me?" Dana shielded her eyes as the curtains were snapped back. Leona, her grandmother's loyal personal assistant, had added waking Dana up to her list of duties.

"Shouldn't have had that party last night. For heaven's sake, it's the middle of the week."

Dana got up and headed for the bathroom. While she washed up, she knew that Leona would wait to ensure her obedience. Loyal to a fault. Dana saw no need to rush toward the eye of the hurricane. She'd get her butt chewed out whether she was one minute late or an hour late.

"Okay, I'm presentable." Dana spun around and modeled as if she was in an exclusive boutique. These days, her outfit was one black or navy pantsuit after another, with an occasional dress or skirt tossed on when she got bored.

"That's better. As usual, you clean up well." Leona sighed. "Thank goodness for that small gem. Time to survey the damage of your festivities." The middle-aged woman even dressed like her boss, in a tailored dark skirt suit and polished black pumps.

Dana saluted Leona, who led the way down the hallway and then marched down the stairs. Since last night's party, the guests had dwindled, but a few sleeping hangers-on were still slumped over wherever they'd crashed. It didn't take much for her small cottage to feel overrun.

Her housekeeper would sweep them out as she did her midweek cleanup. The woman had no patience for "lazy young people." Dana was sure that she was included under that tab, but her leverage was that she paid her housekeeper a salary, and a darn good one.

"Why is Grace up so early?" Dana asked, as Leona continued toward the main house. Her grandmother hadn't wanted Dana to refer to her as "Grandma" once Dana had begun working at Meadows Media and quickly moved up into the higher ranks of the company. The rule was in place—unless Dana knew that she'd crossed the line with a major screwup. Then, she'd slip back to the safety of their unique relationship and call her "Grandma."

For five years, Grace had raised Dana when her mother, Grace's youngest daughter, Elaine, stayed true to her bohemian lifestyle and dumped Dana off to run away on a self-improvement jaunt.

"Business reports are in. The board of directors' annual meeting is in a couple months." Leona glanced over her shoulder to drive home the point.

"I know that much. Is that what's bugging her?"

"She's been agitated about everything ever since she made the decision to celebrate her milestone birthday with a blowout party. It's like she's obsessing about getting her house in order. Getting you in order."

"Why doesn't she wait to see if someone will plan the party? That's how it usually works." Dana ignored the rest of the message.

Leona shrugged, but her expression spoke volumes. Waiting for the other Meadows family members to do anything in a united fashion would be a waste of energy. The Meadows women were known for high drama.

"I have an important meeting later today, so this can't be a walk to the executioner, right?"

Leona threw Dana an amused glance before opening the door to the Meadows mansion.

Dana entered feeling like a gladiator stepping into the Colosseum. The house had been a major part of her childhood and remained an anchor in her adulthood. It also served as her prison when she'd gotten uppity and had been grounded.

Her grandmother was frugal with certain things. No matter what decorated the walls and each room, the overall atmosphere was the same: it was a stately home to invited guests, but for several years, it had been a place of refuge for Dana. When her life had felt out of control, these walls added needed stability.

"Good to see that you look decent." Grace had entered her office, where Dana had waited for her.

"Good morning, Grandma," Dana greeted in as perky a voice as she could muster before she had had her morning coffee.

"When are you going to stop these silly parties? You're getting too old to keep playing at being the popular girl." Her grandmother motioned for her to sit as she pulled out her own chair behind the large desk.

Dana shrugged. "I felt the need to celebrate. Like you with your eightieth birthday."

"I'm celebrating a milestone. What exactly is yours? How many tequila shots you've consumed? Notches on the bedpost?"

"Grandma, that's not nice! And I certainly don't want to talk to you about that last one." Dana's ears flamed over the not-too-subtle criticism. "I'll be ready for the directors' meeting. I promise."

"I'm sure you will, because you have a habit of waiting until the last minute to make an impression. Then, once you squeak by to catch up and ready to work, you're all smiles and witty comebacks, as if you had it under control. You're not fooling me. I want to see you working beyond what's necessary. And stop with the shortcuts and half-assed attitude. The company won't survive with that approach."

"Yes, ma'am." Dana couldn't argue with the obvious. Her grandmother had watched her every move ever since Dana had moved from a general management position a year ago and started the upward climb to her current acting CEO post.

Many observers and industry analysts had thought the creator of Meadows Media would never retire. She was going to be eighty and, until recently, still clocked in a full day's work.

Grace's passion for her company was never in doubt. So it was a shock when she announced her plans, citing family reasons. Despite the retirement announcement, the landscape of Meadows Media sometimes looked as if Grace was still working full time at the company. According to Grace, she wasn't leaving unless certain conditions were in place, namely making Dana, her youngest granddaughter, capable of running the company.

Dana hadn't ever held any doubts about her own future. From the time she started high school, Dana had been coaxed and encouraged to think of Meadows Media as hers one day. Her bachelor's degree in business administration and master's in media management solidified where she would intern and eventually work. While some of her peers worried about finding a job after graduate school, Dana didn't have that burden. Maybe she took it for granted, she'd admit to that, but working for her grandmother hadn't been an easy feat. If anything, she had to work harder and prove herself even more. Her grandmother had mountain-high standards. But the bar was also set by others who measured Dana's few successes and many failures against Grace's iconic accomplishments.

"Now, I will do something that I should have done from the beginning of your term as acting CEO." Grace lightly fingered the pin that she wore on her lapel. The gold feathered pin had no real significance, except to serve as a calming tool when her grandmother had reached that annoyed-to-angry stage. For Dana, the pin was an important signal.

"What's that?" Dana was a bit afraid of her grandmother's solutions. They tended to feel like punishment.

"I'm not sure whether to make it a surprise or if I should

tell you in advance. Of course, knowing you, I suspect that you'd find ways to sabotage these learning opportunities."

"With that introduction, could you blame me?" Dana wracked her brain for a clue from the information she knew.

The older woman's face remained impassive. Time, just shy of eighty years, had been kind to Grace's face. Not that her grandmother didn't look like a senior citizen. She didn't try to hide her age or the natural lines and folds along her features with thick makeup. Her hair, which she wore in her trademark, pinned-up bun, had a healthy helping of gray along the temples, but there was still a significant amount of raven-black color.

Her once erect posture had now bowed at the shoulders. Yet her physique still had a quiet power which she bore with her chin held high, while peering down her nose with strong disdain for people's B.S. Generally, being in Grace's presence tended to keep people on their toes.

"Remember the name Kent Fraser. And that's all I'm going to say. Now, let's go eat breakfast. Then we'll go to the office. I'm meeting with the lifestyle editor and I want your input."

Dana followed. Clearly Grace wasn't going to tell her what brilliant idea she'd cooked up with this Kent person.

They entered the smaller of the two dining rooms. Dana waited for her grandmother to sit before taking her seat. There were no formal rules, but everyone in the clan always deferred to Grace, the matriarch of the Meadows family.

Dana watched the flurried activity of the maid entering and exiting the room, busy with her morning tasks. She figured that her grandmother did most of this for effect, to show that she was still in control. The sparse meal sitting in front of Grace was a boiled egg and a bowl of oatmeal.

In the company of Grace's light fare, Dana never pigged out; instead, she had a fruit salad and a yogurt.

However, when she ditched her grandmother at the office, she'd head out for a big lunch.

"Why are you meeting with the lifestyle editor?" Dana wondered how many others were meeting with Grace.

"She had an idea about doing a follow-up on the kids who survived the Hurricane Katrina destruction. Kind of a where-are-they-now? piece."

"And she didn't feel that she could bring the matter through the current channels?"

"Now, now, don't get your nose out of joint. I was having lunch with a few of the department heads when you were in New York, including Lauren Kirby, who's the polar opposite of O'Brien. He's an acquired taste, don't you think? She mentioned that she had a germ of an idea. We hashed it out until she had a rough draft. Now she's ready to run the entire thing past me for my final input. Then she'll bring it to you."

Dana didn't hide her irritation. "By then, it's too late. You've already given it your blessing." Until she had a sure footing in the company, she planned to copy Grace's style. As acting CEO, Dana oversaw all the departments, with a more hands-on approach for the family-oriented magazine, which had been the backbone of Meadows Publishing, now Meadows Media.

"Not at all. If you don't like it, then don't give it the green light." Grace shrugged. Ambivalence didn't become her. Dana recognized that her grandmother was giving her a dose of her own "whatever" behavior.

"Right. Like I'm going to go on record turning down a Grace Meadows brainchild."

Her grandmother looked at her and then returned her attention to the bowl of oatmeal. She downed several spoonfuls before wiping her mouth. "You, as usual, are being ridiculous."

Dana bit back her reply. She could never win an argument. Not that her grandmother was an excellent debater. Instead, she could be horrendously stubborn. Hashing over the finer details of the reporting chain would be a waste.

"I'm done." Dana had barely touched the fruit salad. When she was around Grace, she wanted eggs, bacon and hash browns. Large helpings of comfort food to ease the stress.

"The car will be around to pick us up in a few minutes."

"I can drive. I want to drive."

Grace paused, clearly not pleased with her choice.

Dana pushed back her chair and headed for the door. This time, she didn't wait for her grandmother to stand. She'd been hit with enough that she needed space and whatever time she had on the drive to work through the myriad of things flitting around in her mind, including Grace's surprise "learning opportunity" with Kent what's-his-name.

Dana relished driving into the office—alone. Her grandmother, on the other hand, liked her perks of a chauffeur. Maybe when Dana got up there in years, she'd give up some of her independence to someone who spent his entire day waiting to drive her wherever she wished. Right now, she needed the extra quiet time to ready her mind for the corporate world.

A half hour later, she pulled into the underground garage. The Meadows Media headquarters was a beautiful piece of architecture and a proud part of the city's upstate New York skyline. The office was built almost thirty years ago when the race to the sky was in full effect with skyscrapers. They had not only built up, but also out, as the Meadows-owned corporation expanded into the family entertainment business with TV, magazine, and radio divisions.

Against this backdrop, Grace had signaled her retirement with the expected announcement of Dana taking over as acting CEO. The official hand-off was expected to occur at the board's meeting, but the minor rumblings of other candidates hoping for the position wore down Dana's nerves. It didn't help that, during the transition, Grace maintained a heavy presence in the office. It was rare that a day went by without her regal march through the office, as if her letting go was only a figment of her employees' imaginations. Dana thought that today happened to be a bit more intense since her grandmother had a mission of sorts. Not once had Grace offered her granddaughter any guaranteed reassurance that the job would be hers. That fact unsettled Dana more than she let on.

"Good morning, Dana. Your schedule and notes are on your desk, along with your coffee."

"Thanks, Sasha." Dana headed into her office and aimed for her desk. Her schedule was a fluid document that started with a few appointments and, by midday, had Dana engaged in one meeting or another.

"Ah, just so you know…Grace has added a few meetings to your schedule."

Dana's hand paused over the keyboard. Her schedule filled the PC monitor. Obviously she couldn't prevent Grace from gluing her butt to the throne she'd built. This interference with her schedule was a bit much. Dana gritted her teeth and bit back her anger.

Sasha was perceptive, though. In a lot of cases, she was the bearer of office news, a one-way flow of information. This prickly situation between Grace and Dana was one subject that was off-limits for discussion.

Dana's finger scrolled down the list of appointments.

She checked the time at the bottom of the monitor screen. The first added meeting was only a few minutes away. Details listed under each appointment didn't include Grace as an attendee. *Small blessings.* Having Grace attend her meetings was nerve-wracking. It was why she partied, to release the pressure valve.

The possibility of becoming the CEO and president was always out there in the periphery. Not close enough to feel real.

Little more than six months ago, Grace had reeled in the leash with little warning that preparation for the role of a lifetime would begin in earnest. The days of walking out without telling her assistant and not returning until the end of the day to then go off and hang out were over. *Time to find a quiet place to think,* was how she justified those midday absences. Now, those absences grew less frequent and the long hours into the evening spent in the office added up.

Last night, as Dana tiredly looked over the freeloaders in her house, she had come to the conclusion that she did want this job—not the current job, as acting CEO—but the full-blown title of president and CEO of Meadows Media. She might not look like a true blue leader right now, but she wanted to be one because she knew this business and she loved the company, but, more importantly, she loved her grandmother.

"Dana, you've got a call from Sean—" Sasha had answered her phone.

"Hang up on him."

"He's downstairs."

"Send him up." Dana raised her hand. "No. Wait."

Sasha froze and waited for her next directive. Her perceptive hazel eyes took in her boss's distress.

"I'll go down to meet him."

"Do you want me to call you and say that you have a meeting?"

"Give me ten minutes. If I'm not up here, send in the cavalry." Dana had no doubt that she'd take care of business before Sasha had to institute Plan B.

"Cool."

Dana chuckled at Sasha's exuberance. Now her assistant might have to bail her out of a personal jam. Between Grace, Leona, and Sasha, she appeared to be unable to handle both the professional and personal areas in her life.

Dana headed to the elevators and rode the cab while rehearsing how she could cut Sean loose. One thing she had to do was stop inviting him back into her life, even as escort to the shindigs she attended. Her only reason for being with him was boredom. Nothing about him held her interest. He used to be the life of the party, knew all the exclusive spots where being a socialite wasn't enough to get her in. As time marched on, she had grown up and his appeal got more wilted around the edges

She emerged into the lobby, scanning the faces of incoming personnel and visitors. He couldn't get through security without a pass or authorized instruction left at the front desk. She walked toward the holding area. There he was, looking disheveled and pale. Crashing on her couch after the party may have helped his drunken state, but he looked like he could have slept for another three hours. No doubt her housekeeper had done the sweep-out and included him in it.

"What do you want, Sean?" Dana motioned him over to the side and out of the way of nosy company employees.

"I...woke up...sorry for bringing all those people. Gosh, I want you." Sean grinned, sheepish but hopeful.

"Got to give it to you. You've got a brass pair. You

wanted to impress your friends and acted like the host all night long."

"I acted like we're a couple." He blinked, his face taking on a dreamy appearance. "We were once."

"Once. A year is enough time to get over it." Dana moved closer to him. He perked up, trying to stand straighter.

"Baby, you are on your way up. You'll need someone at your side who knows you. Who can be there for you." He wiped his forehead, which prickled with sweat.

"Someone who can mooch off of me, right?" Dana had tolerated Sean and his weaknesses because he previously hadn't pushed for anything more than friendship.

"A few mistakes. I'll get back on my feet."

The more he talked, the more sure she was. Sean was her past. She didn't look back, as a general rule, and not for her men. He had all the attributes of a pretty boy. Memories of those glory days, when he was a stockbroker and she was just a socialite, were stuck in his current mindset. Even then, when it was all laughter and champagne, he was cotton candy with no umph.

She slipped her arm through his. He relaxed. A grateful, bleached-white smile popped against his overly tanned skin. They exited the building to stand on the sidewalk, still busy with foot traffic.

"Sean, you need to move on." She raised her hand and a cab swung toward the front of the building. Dana opened the back door and motioned for him to enter. "Where are you heading?"

"What?"

"Who are you shacking up with?"

"Um…ah…"

"Don't worry. I'll pay the cab fare. Your last freebie on my dime, by the way. This is goodbye."

"2000 Silver Birch Terrace."

Dana repeated the familiar address for the cab driver. "Tell your mom I said hello."

She slammed the door closed and, for added effect, brushed her hands together, as if ridding herself of grime.

Dana walked back into the building, stopping by the security booth to instruct them that Sean Lassiter was never to be allowed in the building again. With that, she entered the elevator as her phone rang with Sasha's name popping up to bail her out. No need. She'd managed to clear herself of baggage with no regrets.

Chapter 3

Dana scanned her schedule again, noticing the additional appointments courtesy of Grace. Apparently this was going to be the modus operandi for the foreseeable future. Or until she begged her grandmother to stop. Instead of the usual morning meeting with the department heads, she now had to meet Kent Fraser, an executive coach from England. Sasha had quickly searched for him on the internet and provided Dana with the results.

"Kent Fraser." The name sounded like an uptight, British snob stuck in the days when airs and grace mattered. She snorted.

Was he going to whip her into shape like Audrey Hepburn's classic character? Take her from rags to riches? Fool the masses with his skills? Good luck with those plans. She didn't need that sort of help.

"He's here." Sasha rushed into her office. "I went down to meet him." Sasha was known for her perky demeanor, an abundance of smiles, doelike, expressive eyes, a mop of spiral locks. Today she had been reduced to a giggling, blushing young woman, as if she was on her first date.

"Why? He could have found his way up here."

"Grace suggested that…"

Dana raised her hand. "Never mind." Who on earth was this man that had her staffers stumbling over themselves for him? "Where is he now?" She looked behind Sasha, wondering if her doors would be flung open wide and the great one would walk through to the sound of trumpeters.

"He made a pit stop."

"So he's human after all."

Sasha looked at her with a frown as if she had blasphemed.

Dana decided to *try* to play nice. "Show his lordship in when he returns to your desk."

"Hi, there. Thought that I'd save Sasha the trouble and show myself in. Hope you don't mind."

Dana's pen dropped from her fingertips. Her admiration for him—and it was most certainly such a feeling—started at the top of that slim, trim and damn fine figure of a man. He approached her desk and she swore she heard a voice-over at a fashion show describing the intricacies of his sleek, fitted business suit. Not only did he have drop-dead good looks like a model, he had a vibe that enticed, lassoed and hooked its victim. Kent's easy, casual confidence gave the impression that he was comfortable in his luscious brown skin.

Didn't mean that she didn't appreciate what stood before her. What she'd expected and what stood before her were miles apart. Maybe she should have done her homework and checked up on more than his credentials. But she'd been so sure that her grandmother had dug out a fossil to work with her that she hadn't bothered with the finer details.

Dana smoothed the front of her dress, feeling that she didn't measure up to his polished persona. Her assessment took it all in, but lingered on his face. She couldn't help it. He returned her gaze equally without any shyness.

"Kent Fraser, at your service."

"Dana Meadows." She'd keep to herself what and how she wanted to be *served* by this posh British brother.

"I'll leave you two." Sasha backed out of the office, as if turning her gaze away from him would rob her of something vital.

"Mr. Fraser, would you like coffee…or tea?" Did all British hunks drink tea?

"Coffee. Black, no sugar, please."

Dana nodded to Sasha, who lingered in the doorway. She knew her assistant would get Dana her usual smoothie choice. She returned her attention to her new coach. Yes, she had accepted her fate, with a new verve.

"Since we'll be working together, please call me Kent. And I'll call you Dana."

Looked as if his confidence matched his good looks.

"Will Grace be joining us?"

"No. Have you known my grandmother for a long time?"

"I first met her several years ago when I worked for another firm that was a client. Things didn't go well between the firm and your grandmother, who ended her relationship with my client. Then our paths recently crossed again when I was attached to another firm and we reconnected at a business dinner."

Dana nodded. Terminating a contract sounded like her grandmother. Her reputation as a demanding boss was equal to her notoriety for being a sharklike businesswoman. No one dared cross her and survived to tell the tale. Dana didn't know if she had it in her personal arsenal to approach situations with that keen edge.

"Almost immediately, she approached me to work with her on a consultative basis. Then, upon her recommendation, I got more clients. What I have today is in large part due to her influence and support."

Alarm bells rang on hyper-alert. This man who was hired to "help" her was not just a random person plucked out of the network. His loyalty clearly was aligned with Grace. What Dana did, what she said, how she reacted would all be transmitted in his reports.

Dana re-erected the walls that had crumbled a bit when Kent entered her office. She'd been willing to give him the benefit of the doubt, looking forward to an objective ally of sorts.

"What's next, Kent? Or will you tell me on a need-to-know basis?"

Kent read people. It was his job. From the no-nonsense security at the reception area downstairs to Sasha, the assistant, to Dana Meadows, he read them all. He didn't jump to judgment, but simply filed the details away as he continued to assess. Fixing problems didn't happen overnight. Most times, working with executives required observation, proposals and remedies that he'd constantly tweak to accommodate the client's personal style.

From the instant that he saw Dana, he recognized wariness in her. She visibly withdrew as he explained his connection with Grace, and he couldn't determine the cause yet. The problem didn't influence his approach, except to make him a little more careful with getting Dana to open up about herself and her vision.

He looked forward to the immediate task. How could

he not, when his client was a sensible beauty? His mother had coined that term for women with brains and looks.

Not too often did he have an attractive client to distract him. In those cases, the woman was all window dressing with no substance. A buzzkill for his tastes. Sitting primly in front of him was *that* substance in style and grace. He tried not to be affected by her beauty, which turned Dana into a triple threat against his defenses.

Grace hadn't given him a deadline, but he suspected that there was a short window. It was not a secret that Grace wanted to remove herself completely from the administrative functions of the company that she had created. It was also no secret that the heir apparent who sat in front of him had the momentum to become the next CEO and president.

But obviously Grace wanted to do her bit to ensure that her granddaughter was skilled enough to take on the large responsibility. What Grace had started over thirty years ago was vastly different from where the company was now. It was a more complicated operation and deserved another thirty years of milestones.

"I know you're a busy woman. I'm going to get straight to the point. I will perform an assessment of you, your approach, an analysis of the company. Sort of a case study of you and those around you."

Dana nodded. He noted her constant nervous adjustment of the collar of her dress.

"Toward the end of our time together, I do have a retreat boot camp where you'd be invited to participate with other executives. I think it's important that you have a tight network of alliances for when I step out of the picture."

"And when will you be out of the picture? Is this all mandatory?"

"That will depend on you. Your cooperation." Kent hoped that the time frame wouldn't be too short. Not that

Dana would need major assistance. He just needed time to get to know his subject. All he knew right now was how gorgeous she was—rich brown skin, smooth with bold features, with strength in the heart-shaped face. And that wasn't enough to quench his thirst to know more.

"And what about Grace?"

He remained noncommittal. Again, the mention of Grace caused a switch in her emotion. As quick as a blink, her mouth tightened, then relaxed. No other facial muscle twitched, except maybe the outer corner of her right eye. The handing over of family businesses was a difficult process, many times an unsuccessful one. Infighting and divided loyalties of current staff had the power to create a mutinous atmosphere. He'd be disappointed if that was the case here. He liked and respected Grace.

"Where are you staying?" she asked.

"At Grace's."

"What?"

He laughed at her horrified reaction. "Just kidding."

"Not funny." Although a smile tugged at her mouth, just where a small dimple peeked out.

"I'm staying at the Shelton. I don't like dealing with a commute, whether in London or anywhere else in the world. Besides, I do enjoy walking. Gives me time to think."

Dana nodded. "What about your other clients?"

"I'll be traveling back and forth. I do have a capable staff that assists me. But I'm interested in expanding my expertise into the U.S. markets, which is why I think that I popped up on Grace's radar."

Sasha knocked at the open door and brought in the beverages. He glanced at the green, frothy concoction that Sasha offered to Dana.

Was she a health nut? Someone focused on her image?

A lover of green, disgusting drinks? He'd figured her for the frothy latte type—rich and indulgent.

"I know you'll have some tough questions for me. Let's get that out of the way first." A small green moustache arched over her mouth. The spinach-green against red luscious lips was a nice combo. Her tongue peeked out to wash it clean like an effective wiper blade.

Now he hoped that they stayed here long enough for her to finish the ghastly drink, just for the occasional emergence of her delicate tongue.

Kent swallowed to stamp out a spike of desire. "I would like to submit a 360-degree questionnaire."

"Okay." Despite her assent, she looked decidedly uncomfortable.

"There isn't a fail or pass grade. Only a tool to figure out your strong points."

"I have a feeling that you'll be focused on the weak points. Else, you'd be out of a job."

"I don't look for what's not there. I don't create my tasks." Kent didn't resent the innuendo. Sometimes, just gaining the trust of his client was the hard part. Once they understood and bought into his expertise, working on the improvements was that much easier.

Dana wasn't ready to accept him, though. He knew that and planned accordingly.

"Will I know when the questionnaire is issued?"

"No." The survey had already been administered to everyone, except Sasha and Dana. He didn't quite expect Sasha's candid feedback, but, still, it would be better than nothing. As for Dana, now that he'd met her, he expected that she'd answer with the running thought of how the answer reflected on her professional abilities.

"Are you going to be tagging along? At the company?"

"Sometimes. I have signed a contract with a confidentiality clause."

"We'll take your presence on a case-by-case basis." Her tone hardened to match her distinct displeasure at the idea that he would be around her staff.

Kent had no desire to push his cause. He hoped to gain her trust naturally, albeit quickly. Once her suspicious mind-set broke, she wouldn't see him as the enemy.

He'd sat by the side of many formidable CEOs and business mavericks, young and old. Breaking their trust, abusing the confidant position, those were career-enders. He was damn proud of his reputation and would protect it.

Kent continued, "I'll send you and Sasha the link to the electronic questionnaire. Once you've completed it, we can begin. I'd like to sit in on your department heads meeting. You had one today that was cancelled?"

"Due to your appointment on my schedule."

Kent ignored the accusation. "As soon as you know when the meeting will be, please let me know so that I can set my calendar."

"It will be on Friday afternoon."

"Great. Are you free for lunch today?"

"What else is there to discuss?"

"You."

"Me?" Another sip of the green noxious drink. Another flick of the tongue. Another spike of desire.

"Knowing your personal views and interests will help me."

"This is like having an annual exam."

"Against your will, I know. My apologies."

Dana blew out a frustrated breath. "In a manner of speaking."

"I can promise all day long that I don't mean any harm. That I have the necessary credentials and experience to help. That I will be out of your life as soon as we're done. And despite Grace hiring me, I'm working with you." He stood and extended his hand to her for the second time that day. The second time to see if what he'd felt the first time had actually happened.

His declaration thawed the ice between them. She also stood and offered a wide smile with a firmer handshake. He took the improvement as a sign of progress. What he didn't expect was the stronger buzz through his body at the touch of her hand. Usually he was direct with his gaze, but looking into the dark pools of her eyes had consequences. Normally, he could maintain control of the situation. What she did to his nervous system unnerved him.

What had happened to his cool, emotional detachment?

Instead, his body might as well have walked through a heating vent. He acknowledged the desire stirring awake within him and prayed that he could keep it concealed for more than one day.

The edge of his control grew shaky and unstable. The source of his potential undoing stood in front of him surrounded by a delicate perfume scented with citrus and spice. His gaze drifted from Dana's face down the front of her dress, whose dark color emphasized her femininity, hourglass shape, and added to the image of strength and power.

"Lunch at one o'clock, Kent. Meet me at McCormick's. Sasha will give you the address."

Kent nodded and left. Outside the building, he took a few deep breaths to clear his mind and nostrils of her soft, alluring scent. Mixing business with pleasure was not in his vocabulary. He wasn't the type to be led by sexual urges. But when he had drafted those rules, it didn't take into account the rare find of someone like Dana. She was an intriguing model of contradictions between her stiff, businesslike behavior and his perception of her as a beautiful woman. While she may be wary of him as an interloper, he was afraid that he'd brush aside business decorum to fancy much more from her.

A woman with brains was sexy as hell. A woman with spunk sparked more than casual interest. A woman who drank nasty green potions, well, those belonged to a special grouping.

Kent strolled back to his hotel suite to work on other business. Hands stuffed in his pocket, he almost whistled as he looked forward to his new project.

Dana stood at her office window with her arms folded, looking down at traffic. She had remained in the office on the back side of the floor layout. Back when her grandmother still ran the operations, Dana had wanted to be out of eyesight. Now that she was poised to be named CEO—unless there were enough negative reviews from the business pundits—she would be expected to move into Grace's office with its grand view and presidential-worthy square footage. Dana knew she was a creature of habit that reluctantly viewed change as a good thing.

"Kent Fraser, have you got your work cut out for you?" Dana looked out at the tip of the Shelton hotel building.

"Excuse me?"

"Oh, Sasha, I didn't hear you come in. Please make an appointment at McCormick's for two at one o'clock."

"Um…"

"What is it?" Dana recognized Sasha's reluctance to deliver less than stellar news.

"Your grandmother…Grace…wants to have lunch with you and Mr. Fraser."

"Did she just contact you?" Dana returned her attention

to the view below on the street. Her jaw worked in tandem with her irritated nerves.

"Yes. She will only pop in on your lunch, say a few words and leave. Her words, not mine."

Dana nodded. She returned to her desk to resume working on her latest projects—a magazine theme for the Christmas holidays, the pros and cons of having a satellite radio station, and tossing around the idea of interviewing staff members' families for a round of promotional pieces for the company's TV station.

What could she do about Grace's impromptu appearance at lunch? So far, Dana was the puppet bending and marching to her commands. This learning opportunity definitely had her dragging her feet toward the edges of her comfort zone.

She took a deep breath to calm the impulse to scream. There was an upside.

Maybe having Grace at the lunch would put a coolant on the mysterious sparks that popped up in her, unbidden and out of control, when she was in Kent's company. Dana was mature enough to acknowledge that she was attracted to his looks, attitude and that damned British clipped accent. What she wasn't sure about was whether she could rein in her impulse to flirt and to engage in harmless tomfoolery to feel a bit in control. If she went that route, she could be committing career suicide. The tawdry headlines would add that dig to all the other ways that she didn't measure up to Grace.

But Grace was no angel, either.

Part of the Meadows family drama revolved around past hurts and long-ago disagreements that Grace had orchestrated, participated in or was guilty of by association. In addition to having Dana take over Meadows Media, her grandmother had plans to task her with making sure every family member would attend her eightieth birthday. Only death was an excuse and then, Dana knew, Grace would probably want a written note from the Man above.

"Miss Meadows!" Dana looked up at the man who had burst through her door, with Sasha bringing up the rear in a blustery rush.

"O'Brien." No matter how many times she told Peter O'Brien, head of advertising, to call her Dana, he refused. Once, he cited that he'd have to get to know her and feel comfortable before he did that. How could she argue with that logic?

"Did you have the department heads' meeting without me?" He glared down at her. Suspicion was a steady companion with Peter.

"No, I did not."

"I tried to tell him that." Sasha didn't hide her irritation.

"I would like to talk to you…alone." He turned an icy glare at Sasha and gestured toward the door.

Her assistant was no wilting flower and his high-handed behavior turned her usual doe-eyed expression hard.

"No offense," he remarked, his attention back on Dana.

"Offense taken." Sasha wasn't backing down.

"Sasha, please excuse us." Dana tried to convey to Sasha that she'd handle his rudeness. One battle at a time. Her assistant left, but Sasha's mouth was pinched as if she could barely keep herself from saying something that she'd regret.

The office door clicked shut. Dana waited a beat before she addressed her angry visitor.

"I want to make my position very clear. I have been an integral part of Grace's team for many years." Peter's hands cut through the air to emphasize his point. "I still have a lot to offer this company. I know that you will come in with your own ideas and have your own team—"

"Stop right there!" Dana rubbed her temples. "Have a seat. You're making my neck hurt looking up." She waited until he responded to her request. "First, the meeting was cancelled because, believe it or not, things come up. An email went out to all who had accepted the meeting request." She clasped her fingers to force herself to keep her tone even. "You are a valuable employee of the company. What you have done for Grace, I expect you to do under my leadership. Where we go from here is based on a mutual commitment and respect. I don't care to be approached with a level of aggression that is not only annoying, but disrespectful."

"I didn't mean—"

"I'm not finished speaking. I don't appreciate you treating Sasha or any member of my staff with contempt. Got it?"

"Yes, ma'am."

"You will get an updated appointment for the department heads' meeting. I suggest that you make sure to accept the calendar request when it comes through your email. Now, I have another meeting to get to, if you don't mind." Dana sat back in the chair. Whether he was done or not, she was cutting the meeting short. At another time, when tempers had cooled, they could have a more civil conversation where he could air his grievance. Right now, Peter needed to be put in his place.

She knew people would test her like a substitute teacher in a high school. Well, bring it.

A few minutes later, a soft knock at her door interrupted her. She suspected who it could be. "Hi, Sasha," she greeted her assistant, whose head poked through the doorway.

"He apologized." Sasha covered her mouth, but a giggle escaped.

"Good."

"Thank you."

"It's nothing more than I would expect from anyone, including you. Besides, I'm counting on you to be instrumental with keeping us moving forward in accord with one another." Dana beckoned her into the office.

Sasha entered and sat on the edge of the chair.

"You have earned a promotion to the position of office administration manager, for which I'm happy to sign off. I will make the announcement at the department heads' meeting. Although I am your direct supervisor, this promotion has the backing of various departments, including O'Brien's. Regardless of any insecurities people might have with me at the helm, they are one hundred percent supportive on the great job you do."

Sasha beamed at the accolades.

Dana handed her the official letter from Human Resources, along with the salary increase notification. "It is retroactive to the beginning of the month."

"Oh, my gosh. I didn't expect this." Sasha clutched the letter to her chest. Her eyes glistened as she swallowed her rising emotions.

"It is my pleasure." Dana refrained from adding that Sasha might regret the new classification when she saw the level of her assignments and tasks. "Because you will be working on strategic tasks which will pull your attention from the mundane ones, you will have a junior assistant to help you and to take on my more administrative responsibilities."

"Oh." Now Sasha sat up straighter.

"We can put our heads together to find the ideal candidate. I'll do the final interviews, but you and HR can run with the first-round candidates. And I'd like this done sooner rather than later."

"Yes, ma'am."

"Oh, goodness, please do not go all *O'Brien* on me."

They shared a laugh. The idea of promoting Sasha didn't cause any doubts or hesitation for Dana. To have a right-hand person who could foresee rocky waters and hidden dangerous currents was vital. She didn't need an executive coach to tell her that nugget. Common sense sometimes beat all the highfalutin management B.S. that so-called experts wanted to sell.

"Well, that's it. If you have any questions, I'm here."

"Thanks, Dana. I'm ready for this. You will not regret this one bit."

"My pleasure."

Sasha looked over at the miniature clock on a side table. "Time for your lunch."

Only ten minutes to spare. Chances were that she'd be late. Great. She would not only be late to her meeting with her coach, but would have Grace as a witness.

Nothing to do but haul tail.

Chapter 4

Dana rushed into McCormick's, which was already crowded with the lunch regulars. She didn't have a chance to pull herself together before Grace raised her hand and flicked it, signaling Dana to approach. So much attitude oozed from Grace's one movement and her imperious demeanor. Nonetheless, Dana resisted the urge to hurry to where Grace and Kent were seated. Time to reset the power balance, even if Grace wasn't aware there was a battle of sorts going on.

"Hi, Grace. Good to see you." Dana kissed her grandmother's cheek. The woman could be Diana Ross's twin in looks and Lena Horne in cool sophistication. However, the older woman couldn't sing a lick, although that didn't stop her from trying. Hence, the karaoke machine that Grace had bought for herself last year as a birthday gift.

"Everything at the office okay?" Grace looked pointedly at her watch.

"Yes." Dana turned her attention to Kent who was looking at her with an assessing regard. "Have you all had a chance to catch up?" Dana took the seat next to her grandmother's, but opposite Kent. Seating options were limited—both choices were a burden on her nerves.

"Kent was filling me in on his latest pursuits. I'm so glad that he could squeeze us in his busy schedule." She patted the top of his hand.

Dana almost choked on her glass of water that the waitress had brought over when she sat down. Since when did Grace have a soft spot for anyone? Granted, Dana herself sometimes managed to appeal to her grandmother, but only with a great deal of work and her grandfather's intervention, and after lots of whining. Dana looked at Grace, then Kent. Good grief, she hoped that her grandmother wasn't having a cougar moment. There were many stories floating around the family that Grace was quite the femme fatale. Her exploits were blamed on her great-aunt's spinster state—years ago, Grace had eloped with her sister's fiancé.

Why else would Grace appear all soft and gooey over Kent, who certainly had the "it" factor to grab any female's attention? He was more than just handsome, but really—her grandmother? Laughter bubbled up. She sputtered while taking a sip from her glass of water.

"Are you all right?" Kent asked.

Dana nodded, hiding the smile behind her napkin. "I think it's time to order."

"I'm skipping lunch. Your grandfather is meeting me. We are going to the theater later tonight." Grace turned her full attention to Dana at her side. "One of the things that Kent will be assisting us with is the strength-weakness analysis of the company. He can recommend a great advisor to help with the process. Makes sense in getting a full exam, don't you think?"

"Kent appears to have a lot of skills. From being my coach to analyzing companies." Dana didn't bother to hide the doubt. "Next he'll be our life coach."

Grace tittered. "Kent, have you managed to include those services?"

"I find that Americans tend to overindulge on the counseling approach, if you're to believe those reality shows."

"That was a joke, not to be taken seriously." Dana interrupted before her grandmother and this spin doctor invaded her life any further.

"Might help, though." Grace cocked an eyebrow.

Dana's cheeks burned.

Kent broke in. "The company's analysis will be intense, but can be completed within the month, maybe even shy of that. The survey results will be incorporated in the report. Dana and your company are my sole projects."

"Sounds good to me. Dana, make sure to bring it up in the meeting on Friday. And I also think that you should go to New York City, as soon as you can schedule it, and meet with the various division heads."

Dana nodded.

Within Meadows Media, each business division had different audiences and measurements of success. As CEO, Dana would be expected to have the business chops to manage and make the tough decisions to keep both the headquarters and subsidiaries running. The usual meeting in New York City had decidedly now turned into a major deal, as the final meeting before the board made its decision.

"One component to success that I stress with any CEO is the team," Kent said, more to Grace than to Dana.

"I do have a great team," Grace responded with unmistakable confidence.

"Each leader needs her own team." Kent still kept his attention on Grace.

"And Dana will have a great team when she takes over, with lots of years of experience. No need to upset the apple cart. Don't you agree?" The question hung, pregnant and heavy, in the air.

Dana resumed drinking her water.

Kent looked as if he wanted to attempt to cut the tension between her and her grandmother. She hoped he didn't try to play hero so early in the game. No need to instigate a contest to see whom Grace favored.

Grace continued, unaware or clueless of the uneasiness that resulted in the wake of her announcements. "I also want you to attend the executive retreat in England."

"I thought that was optional. I don't have time to do all this and run a company." The brutally honest sentiment spilled out before Dana could restrain herself.

Grace cleared her throat. "That's why I'm still around."

Dana had taken on the position of acting CEO with full knowledge that her grandmother still had the reins wound around her hands. Once in a while, Dana was allowed to head up a team and run with an idea, but, for the most part, she didn't do anything without first informing Grace. In the beginning, the staff was confused as to whom they should report; they only addressed Dana if Grace sent them her way.

Everyone expected Grace to fully retire any day. Her continued presence at Meadows Media seemed to convey that although Dana had the acting CEO position, there might still be room for someone with better credentials to take the top spot. That possibility created a sharklike infestation in the corporate waters. One slight nick and the hint of blood would draw out the hungry, competitive swarm to take Dana out. What she couldn't figure out was if this was all part of a test Grace created for her. Or did her grandmother truly think that she might not be up to par?

"It's a four-day seminar," Kent offered, this time turning his attention to Dana.

"I don't have a choice."

"Good. Well, that's settled." Grace gathered up her personal items. "I'm going to leave you in Kent's capable hands. I know you have your doubts about him. I want to lay your worries to rest. I'm confident you will find his input invaluable. He's a wonder." Again, she squeezed his hand and offered a rare, bright smile.

Dana was ready to hurl. At least he didn't respond like cougar bait.

"Grace, I appreciate your confidence. Dana *is* in good hands."

Oh, wonderful, now they were talking as if she was ten years old and not in the room. She remained quiet, waiting for her grandmother's exit.

At last, Grace stood and fixed her clothes back into neat order. "Great. I'm glad that your tardiness allowed me a chance to catch up with Kent. I even tried to entice him to stay at the house."

"What?" Dana wanted to bite her tongue for reacting so sharply *and* loudly.

"Thank you for the offer." Kent didn't offer a *but*.

What the hell! Was he considering it?

"Maybe next time." Grace waved and left in a vapor trail of expensive perfume.

Dana turned her attention to Kent. He'd better not take Grace up on her offer. This business arrangement was a tad too cozy. Still, she found herself shifting her chair closer to his in case they decided to talk about confidential business matters. The problem with being in such close proximity to Kent—while trying to think the worst of him—was that it didn't work.

Admiring him up close. Inhaling his cologne. Gazing at his hands and long, tapered fingers. Listening to his voice, deep, smooth, like a stroke across the skin.

Those irritable thoughts about him took a sharp turn toward the land of temptation. From there, her thoughts descended toward an erotic fantasy of epic proportions. Naked abs, a hard, thick arousal. Dark brown bedroom eyes. British-accented, raw sex talk.

Dana drank the remainder of her water. Her body had responded—wet and ready for action.

Kent didn't realize until Grace's departure how much her presence had affected the mood like a barometric reading. Although there was a subtle shift in Dana's body language, he didn't miss how her shoulders relaxed and the pinched expression, especially around her mouth, disappeared. Yet he didn't get the impression that there was animosity between the two. From his outsider vantage point, he saw a proud, protective grandmother hovering, sometimes too close, to a granddaughter who seemed unsure.

He couldn't tell if the CEO position was Dana's calling or if it was a role borne out of expectation.

Today, Grace had stopped dancing around a prickly issue related to his assignment. In his final report, he had to provide his recommendation on whether or not Dana was deemed a good fit for the position of CEO of Meadows Media. The board, made up of family, outside investors, and salaried employees, was unsure and, although Grace had the final say, they did have the power to make the transition a smooth one or a mutinous one. Someone could have all the skills, push the right buttons, step up to be an effective leader. But that wasn't whom Grace wanted to fill her shoes. She wanted someone who couldn't see himself or herself anywhere but in those shoes. All her life, Dana had been groomed. At the end of the day, grooming worked, but only up to a point. The remaining ingredient was passion.

In order for him to get to the passion, though, Kent had to get to know Dana. Really know her. The way her gaze, dark and angry, slashed over him told him that the job would be darn difficult. He waved the waitress over and asked for another glass of water with lemon. Once Dana gave her order for some type of tofu salad, Kent provided a selection that was at the opposite end of the caloric range. Something told him this job would test his skills, his patience, and his good sense.

As Dana drank her replenished water, all he saw was the motion of her throat as she swallowed. He followed the slender length to the small opening V at the top of her dress that showed off the indentation at the base of her throat. The garment's silky top molded smoothly to her shoulders and arms. He'd be a hypocrite if he didn't admit to admiring how it also thinly shielded the swell of her breasts.

When the waitress approached with his small bowl of chicken noodle soup, and later his burger, Kent almost popped up out of his seat to meet her halfway for his food and Dana's. Any distraction was desirable to snap the strange mood created by this delicate link between him and Dana.

"That looks…interesting." *Inedible* was more like what he was thinking when he saw her tofu, spinach and eggplant meal. There were other wilted green leaves that didn't quite look like lettuce. And the colorful combination of ingredients didn't match the seemingly boring nature of her dish. Again, Kent wondered if Dana was a health nut, not that he minded. He was quite pleased with the results.

"This is a special greens mix that the chef has made. Full of antioxidants."

"Mmm." He bit into his burger and relished the juice that spilled out. While Kent was visiting America, he was determined to try as many as possible of the country's celebrated foods, with lots of toppings and tasty condiments. To combat the effects of his eating plan, Kent had scheduled occasional workouts in a gym. He suspected that, after this trip, he'd also have to be nibbling on food fit for a rabbit.

"Would you like to try some?"

"No, thank you." Kent became even more definitive in his dietary goal when the familiar green beverage appeared. If Dana kept drinking this green nonsense, he might never kiss those lovely red lips.

His fork clattered against the plate. "Pardon me. Slipped." Indecision wasn't a part of his genetic makeup. Something as simple as kissing her wasn't about *if* it should happen. Instead, the thought, appearing clear and brash in his mind, only prompted the question of *when* the kiss would occur. Once this job was done, he had every intention of engaging in a romantic liaison with Miss Meadows.

"I hope that I don't make you nervous." Her dimple winked at him.

"Not at all." *Once this job was done.*

"What do I make you feel?" she asked after chewing on the leaves.

Hard.

"Forget the question. It's actually not important. I don't think you'll be around long enough for it to matter."

"Have everything all figured out, do you?" Kent didn't like being dismissed.

"It's my job to do so."

"Do you see what you do as a job?"

She drained her glass of its hideous contents. "What else is it?" Her tongue did its customary sweep, left to right, leaving her lips moist and wet.

He shrugged. Desire kept turning up his temperature to a squirm-in-the-seat level. "I'm wondering if you're the nine-to-five type, or do you pull all-nighters?"

"If you have a good staff in place, there is no need to pull all-nighters," Dana said. "Grace only works with the best."

"I'm sure Grace pulled all-nighters." Kent wasn't correcting her notion. Grace was known for her workaholic tendencies. Her granddaughter, however, had a tendency to be known for large parties that had people begging to be on the invite list.

Dana leveled a death glare at him. "Everyone has his or her own style…and can still get the job done." She signaled the waitress to the table, flashing her credit card.

"I was planning to get it." The driver's seat was getting mighty small, with both of them jockeying for position.

"Unnecessary. Grace invited us to lunch and skipped. So we could eat and finish whatever preliminary work needed to be done in order for you to proceed."

"In that case, thank you." He leaned back and waited for the waitress to swipe her card on the gadget attached to the check-holder. "I've sent you the survey."

"I saw it as I was leaving. I'll have it to you by tomorrow." Dana looked at her watch. "The department meeting is on Friday. You're coming?"

"Of course." He wanted to see her work with more than just him or Sasha.

"I hope you're not going to act like every move warrants note-taking."

"I do make notes, but not while I'm processing."

"Ah, so this is what *this* is. Processing."

"Yes." Kent didn't care for the smirk that tugged play-fully at her mouth.

"And you don't share your notes." She bit her lip.

"No," Kent answered with emphasis. *No, as in stop bit-ing your lip. He wanted to do that.*

"How about the processing?" Dana asked.

"Sometimes." He knew that he had to offer her feed-back eventually. She knew it, too. "I will share it with you and Grace because it may shape some of the business rec-ommendations."

A shadow of unease flickered over her face, removing any hint of amusement.

"I don't blindside clients." He attempted to reassure her. Making her comfortable was important for him to com-plete his job. However, there was no denying that winning over Dana served his own needs and intentions. That prom-ise to himself, to wait until after the job was done before turning on the charm, steadily rang hollow.

She shrugged. Again, the top of her dress slid up and down over her full breasts. Kent had to work on keeping his gaze averted. He had never gotten thrown off a project before, and he had no doubt that Dana would happily vol-unteer for the opportunity to toss him out on his ear. If he couldn't keep his head together, she might get the chance.

His unusually strong attraction to Dana Meadows put Kent's defenses on alert, especially since he sensed that she was checking him out, too. He needed to build up re-inforcement to stay focused, as soon as possible. Nothing that he couldn't handle.

But in the meantime, if he could only put his hands on her full, curved butt cheeks, he could get it out of his sys-tem. Sometimes, he knew, eradicating something from a diet was worse than sampling tiny portions. Kent licked his lips and tried to push down his arousal before leaving the cover of the table. His abandoned, half-eaten burger had to be sacrificed to the bin.

Chapter 5

Dana would rather run with the bulls in Spain than run the department heads' meeting. Heck, she'd rather cut out of work early and join the Friday happy hour crew than have Kent in observation mode for the next hour. Taking a deep breath, she pulled open the conference room door.

The conference room was filled with Meadows Media's senior management. Dana sat at the head of the table, acutely aware of the staff's unease. She was heading the meeting without Grace for the first time. The staff's glances shifted between her and Kent, who sat in the extra seating area along the outer edge of the room.

Sasha made her way around the room, distributing updated agendas. A few department heads who'd procrastinated with turning in their reports handed their USB sticks to her. Each person seated at the table had to present their weekly reports on their department's work, along with accompanying statistical data in a PowerPoint presentation.

At two o'clock on the dot, Dana cleared her throat loudly and tapped the file in her hands on the table to signal the start of the meeting. Grace should be impressed that she started on time.

"Good afternoon to all of you. Before we get underway, I'd like to introduce Kent Fraser, a consultant, who will be working on business development for Meadows Media."

Everyone looked at Kent, who stood and curtly nodded. Dana didn't miss the women who gave him the once-over. She also didn't miss that they wrote notes on the edges of their agendas and slid them across the table for their female peers to read. The men also appeared to note Kent's good looks, but probably viewed them as some sort of competition. They corrected their postures, straightened their ties, or smoothed their shirtfronts. As a rule, it didn't pay to have a boyfriend who was *too* good-looking. Not that she considered him boyfriend material—too proper, too well-mannered, too subdued. She always had an attraction to a bad-boy type. Kent Fraser didn't have a bad bone anywhere. Maybe if he hung out in America long enough, she could corrupt him.

Dana fanned away the blush that suffused her entire face. There was nothing boyish about this tall, fine man.

Realizing that the attention was back on her, Dana continued, "Please extend Kent any assistance that he may need."

Dana kept her line of vision down the center of the conference table. She wanted to hold it together and not allow any inappropriate thoughts about Kent's intrusion on her professional life or his influence on her private musings. More importantly, she didn't want the evidence of her feelings plastered on her face. It was bad enough that she couldn't hold her tongue when her emotional buttons were pushed. Facial expressions were another hot button that often landed her in delicate situations where she had to apologize and squirm her way out of sticky *faux pas*.

Dana began the presentation, going through the data and her expectations. The numbers didn't lie. Ever since Grace appointed her to the company's helm, the industry watchers had reacted. She had done nothing differently from what Grace would have done. She made sure that her footprint fit squarely and snugly in her grandmother's, not deviating from Grace's example because of the expected scrutiny. Yet she was being questioned every step of the way and blamed for anything that went askew by the business analysts.

"The family and fashion magazines are killing the company," O'Brien piped up. "Advertising is down. Overhead is up. Radio isn't any better."

She saw Kent pick lint off his pant leg. His facial reaction was hidden from her view. "Nothing is killing the company, Peter. We are in the middle of the fourth-quarter numbers. They are slightly below last year's, but it has been that way for the entire year."

"Compared to other similar-sized companies, we're on par. The bad winter hit all the markets hard, driving up costs on supplies, delaying deliveries, and in some cases, destroying equipment." That assistance came from the finance department head.

"You don't play it safe to stay in the business." O'Brien leaned far back in his chair with his hands clasped behind his head. A smirk punctuated his know-it-all expression. "I don't recall such dire numbers last year, or the year previous to that, and the market was worse then."

Dana felt the sharp edge of his challenge. He might think that she was going to waver. Not happening. "Last year, this year, next year, will each have its unique dynamics. Once a strong plan is in place, along with contingencies, there is no need to push the panic button. Otherwise, you might be called an alarmist."

Ruddy pink suffused O'Brien's face. He straightened up in his chair. His fingers furiously twirled a pen and his mouth thinned to the point of disappearing. His withering glare spoke volumes. His mumbling under his breath brought a few chuckles from his immediate neighbors.

"I hate to act like the kindergarten teacher, but, if you have something to share, please do so." Dana waited a few beats until the staff quieted down. "Good. Now, for the report from legal…"

Silence descended.

Some faces registered their shock at her authoritative demeanor. Grace might as well have walked into the room and conducted the meeting. Shocking people into silence was her expertise.

O'Brien wouldn't let up, though. "I simply said that a strong plan is only as good as its leader."

The head of the legal department cleared his throat, but didn't proceed.

O'Brien's continued contempt goaded her to respond.

Hot anger shot a fiery flame through Dana's body. Her hands shook with small tremors over his audacity. All she could see in her anger-constricted vision was his slick, cocky smile. The constant need to defend her rise in the company and her work experience were always triggers for her temper.

And O'Brien was about to get a taste of what it felt like to cross her.

She noticed that Kent shifted his position, folding his arms and breaking eye contact with her. They hadn't known each other long enough to understand one another's body language. From their conversations throughout the week, Dana could figure out his approach. She sensed that he wanted her to power it down. Switch the jets to neutral.

All well and good in theory, but why should she listen to him in the real world? O'Brien's public dressing-down by her was one second away from happening. She'd be justified taking the annoyingly intelligent, but insufferable, know-it-all to task. After all, he basically dissed her in front of the senior management.

Kent coughed softly. This time, he pinned her with a steady gaze from his dark brown eyes. Was he going to hypnotize her into submission? She held on stubbornly for a few seconds.

Fine. She'd lower the gears from a public bloodletting to barely concealed annoyance.

"Thank you for your keen insight, Peter. And, as the leader, I will make sure that we all contribute to building a strong plan." She couldn't rein in the sarcasm. "Let's move on. I don't want this to last all day. Wharton, please proceed with the report from legal." The meeting continued without incident or without descending into a pissing contest by Peter or anyone else.

After the meeting, no one lingered. Dana remained seated. She wasn't going to run out of the room. She maintained eye contact with everyone who passed. O'Brien tried to keep himself insulated within a group of his cronies as he timed his exit.

"Mr. O'Brien, may I speak to you?" Kent spoke.

Dana's attention snapped to Kent. She didn't see that one coming. To pluck the most outspoken member of the herd out for a debriefing didn't sit well with her. O'Brien looked equally uncomfortable, but he had no choice, given Dana's previous endorsement of Kent.

"You may use this room." Dana gathered her stuff and left, pretending as if none it mattered to her.

Now, what would Kent want to know? Was O'Brien one of the sample reviewers? Seeing Kent writing copious notes throughout the meeting unnerved her. Had she been graded? Dana didn't feel that she'd failed, if there was a test. She did back down, wimped out, gave in, per his vibes from across the room. Mr. Executive Coach should be impressed. But she also didn't think that it would be the last time that someone publicly tested her. Once O'Brien set the standard, she could expect others to gain the confidence to be defiant. How was she going to lead when she had to keep an eye on any oncoming threats and for the possible mutiny behind her? What she didn't have, and very much needed, was Grace's backing to create her own team.

Dana waited in her office, wondering when Kent would request to speak to her. An hour later, he still hadn't shown up. The office, which was mostly enclosed by glass, allowed her to see most of the floor space when her blinds were open.

Half an hour later, O'Brien had been released back into the fold. He was walking around, chatting it up with any willing ear. Dana didn't care about him at the moment. Her focus had switched to Kent's whereabouts. Not that she needed to talk to him. His feedback wasn't on the top of her priorities for the afternoon.

Rather than wait for him to wreck the rest of her day, she gathered her stuff and headed out of the office. If she had her way, she'd be heading for home, enjoying a glass of wine, and inviting a friend or two to come over to help her to wind down. Her midweek—and even weekend—house parties had to take a long hiatus. Right now, though, the event for the evening was a private reception at an art gallery.

Some extracurricular activities sucked so badly that she never wanted to attend, or participate in, them. But the art gallery was a major exception. In addition to being a powerhouse in the media and entertainment businesses, Grace had a strong, philanthropic mind-set. Her interests were diverse and wide, ranging from adopting abandoned exotic pets and providing for their care in animal refuges, to offering various grants for community artists to pursue their vocations. Tonight's high-priced fund-raising dinner was one of many events Grace took part in to refill the cultural commission's coffers needed to host the city's annual art festival in the early summer. Another personal connection made it particularly special. The festival was one of the few activities for which both Grace and Dana's mother shared a passion.

When Elaine had reappeared in Dana's life recently, one of the "safe" activities—ones that didn't result in familial acrimony—that she, Dana and Grace could engage in was art appreciation. Her mother, who only dabbled in painting, was a beloved part of the city's artists' community. She introduced Dana to many of the up-and-coming stars of the local art scene. From there, the idea for the fund-raiser was born and she shared it with her grandmother. Dana suspected Grace's enthusiastic support—given without putting up a fight or Dana having to defend the plan—was the only way Grace could enjoy her youngest daughter's company. Their volatile history tended to sabotage the fragile reconnection.

Not too many events would have invited both notable artists from across the country and the world international stage to spend hours at a cocktails and dinner reception with local talents struggling for recognition. Dana knew that everyone needed connections, whether it was to climb the ladder to success or to be mentored by someone with clout.

Unlike some events, which provided an indirect media

spotlight for local politicians, this actual art festival was about community. Dana loved her grandmother's tenacity to stay true to her spirit. She vowed to continue in the same vein at work and with any charity she was involved in.

A significant number of attendees had already arrived at the community art center by the time Dana got there. For tonight, the building had been spruced up with a fresh coat of paint, outdoor decorative plants and a professional touch to turn its interior into an art gallery.

She handed her car keys over to the valet and headed for the entrance. Sticking close to the crowd, she was able to enter without anyone recognizing her. Nowadays, the press had an annoying habit of showing up at the most inopportune times to demand to know if she would be CEO of Meadows Media. When Dana answered in the affirmative, they'd ask when. She shook her shoulders to rid herself of work matters. Tonight, she only wanted to enjoy fine art.

A passing waitress offered her a choice of white or red wine. She gratefully relieved the server of one glass of white and took an appreciative sip.

"Mind if I hang by your side, since I don't know anyone?"

Dana jumped. Kent's voice stroked her entire back. The man must be kinfolk to a genie with his sudden appearances. And if she could have him spin some magic, she'd want that same soulful, British voice to turn into warm caramel syrup that could be poured all over her body.

He casually tapped her shoulder. "Didn't mean to startle you. I just arrived." He scanned the room. "And, of course, I don't know a soul. Well, except for you and Grace. Haven't seen her either."

"I just got here, too." Dana took a couple steps back to add space between them. His cologne did crazy things to her senses. Was this the same effect that cell phones had on airplane controls?

"I saw the Meadows name on the building."

"Grace is very big on the arts." Dana turned into a side room that displayed sculpted pieces. Although she stood in front of each work of art, she couldn't quite split her attention between the frozen shapes and the man next to her, who was very much alive.

Finally, Kent moved off to admire a collection of oil paintings. Keeping an eye on him, she followed his movement to the other side of the room.

A large sculpture dominated the center. The crudely shaped model was of a man with anatomical details that made her wonder about the model's *assets*. What she saw deserved a rating to attract single horny females. The pose didn't help tame her crazy thoughts—a man in a defiant stance, standing tall with legs apart, hands fisted on hips, broad shoulders pushed back to accentuate his chiseled chest, head turned to show off a bold, harsh profile.

The statue appeared to mock her with what she couldn't have. None of her past relationships had had the power to satisfy her sexual appetite. That ten-foot-tall sculpture drove home the point that the guy who would meet her needs could only be a fabricated bronze exhibit that the artist must have embellished.

Only, there might be an exception. *Might* being the operative word. There was no concrete evidence about her very British suspect to prove her intuition. From her vantage point, as she pretended to focus on another sculpture, she saw that Kent had the physical attributes to be this model. Now, as far as the anatomical details, she'd have to see them with her own eyes.

The mental visual caused her to squeeze them shut.

Xray vision would be a worthwhile power to possess.

Then if the examination turned up nothing substantive, she didn't have to imagine, desire or hope for a miracle.

He caught her scrutiny and matched it with his intense look. Damn his sexy mouth. Thin. Wide. An ever-present smirk that made her feel as if he had a personal joke that he wasn't sharing with her.

Dana couldn't break eye contact with him, despite being caught red-handed. Her nimble mind had turned her into a sculptor, one who was skilled with her hands and had a sharp eye for details. If he only knew that she had him in her crosshairs.

Right there, above where his neck stretched out of his shirt, corded muscles provided enough evidence that his upper torso matched his body's lean dimensions. Under the starched white shirt, under the cotton undershirt, she'd discover his pec muscles were toned just enough, but not freakishly so. He didn't sport facial hair, so she'd guess that his chest would be somewhat smooth, allowing her to admire the dark chocolate nipple that dotted the base of each plane.

She flexed her hands, as if she had finished a portion of the sculpture. But she couldn't leave it unfinished without filling in the rest of his midsection. Did he carry four-pack or six-pack washboard abs? Did he have that deep vertical groove on either side of his ribs to encase the taut ab muscles?

Now, she wasn't a muscle fanatic. Kent didn't need to be on the cover of a men's workout magazine in order to set off the rockets in her private parts. What Dana really found sexy about a man was the deep V-shaped muscle that started out wide from the belly button and sloped seductively into the waistband of his pants. Now, that gem did have the power to make her moist.

She licked her lips. Suddenly, her throat was parched.

Where the heck was the waitress? Water, wine, anything to wet her lips. But she wasn't moving to seek hydration.

Time for rendering an anatomically correct reproduction. Dana clasped her hands and cracked her fingers.

"If that look could talk, I suspect that I may not want to hear what it had to say. And that killer smile that you're flashing makes me wary." Kent stepped out of her range of sight.

"Didn't figure you as the type to run." Dana felt the need to stand near the overhead air-conditioning vent. The image of what she'd conjured up took its sweet time evaporating from her mind

"Not running."

"Good. I'm hoping that you don't." She took a deep breath. "There's too much to enjoy here. But I'll understand if you should have to back out early."

"I wouldn't want to disappoint you." Kent continued to walk through the other exhibits.

Every so often, he'd look over his shoulder and send her a small smile that set her nerves into a tailspin of tingling excitement.

Dana couldn't remember the last time she'd flirted with a man. Maybe because few had both the strong sex appeal and brains she was looking for. The more time she spent with him, the more dangerous he was to her self-control. Being around Kent was like a workout—holding in, holding back, suppressing what should be natural. But circumstances and decorum blocked her real inclination—to take a running jump and land on his chest, wrap her legs around him and plant the biggest, wettest kiss on his lips.

Some dreams did come true.

The man made her feel like drooling. Even the way he strolled from exhibit to exhibit had a bad-ass style. He was hot sex on two legs—a prediction, of sorts. She cursed the annoying fact that because he was her coach, he couldn't be a notch on her bedpost, as Grace so bluntly stated.

Dana's flirty, and most certainly horny, side challenged her rational one: *Why the hell not?*

Kent tracked Dana's sultry laughter as she navigated the twists and turns of the gallery space. He deliberately moved through the rooms quickly to keep her out of his sight. Otherwise, he'd lose the small element of self-restraint he had. The sound of her laughter wrapped itself along the walls and lingered, teasing him with its husky, warm tone. She was teasing him, of that he was certain.

Cheeky she-devil.

If he didn't work hard to avoid her influence, she'd wrap him in a web. In Kent's past relationships, no woman had ever sat in the control seat, not for one second. He'd never been attracted to that type. Until now. Regardless of his wayward cravings, he'd have to tamp down on the primal urge to step up and lay claim to Dana. No doubt they would battle for dominance in both their professional relationship and hopefully in any private seduction. A dance that promised to thrill. His physical arousal seconded the thought.

"What now?"

"I think it's time to let Grace know that we're here." Kent didn't expect Dana to cut short their game of cat and mouse. They were back among the other patrons, who were oblivious to the heady pulse of their mutual attraction.

"Yes, our boss lady must be aware of our presence."

They headed over to Grace who reigned over her age-diverse circle of friends. Kent could actually smell the massive collected wealth of these philanthropists. Grace introduced him to her companions and praised his work highly to them.

"I think the only thing left is for you to walk on water," Dana quipped, for his hearing only.

"Can't do that. But I can perform magic tricks."

"I'm sure the woman on the right would love to play your magician's assistant."

"No, thank you." Women attracted to him flattered his ego, but, in the past, some had taken that attraction to a level that seemed a bit unhinged. "Not into the clingy types."

"How about the one on the left? Oh, oh, I think she just winked."

"Nope." Kent didn't bother to check out of any of Dana's recommendations. He had already looked around. No one in the gallery compared to her. So why bother?

"What's wrong with her?" Dana asked.

"I have a thing for feet. She doesn't measure up in those sandals." He shook hands with the next person Grace pushed toward him. Afterward, he turned to Dana. "You would pass that criterion, though."

His compliment froze her in her place. He watched her stare at her feet, which were encased in gladiator-style sandals with a killer heel.

Kent enjoyed having the last laugh. "Good night. See you in the morning."

As he exited, he heard the sound of someone hurrying behind him. Without turning, he sensed that Dana had followed him. He slowed to allow her to catch up. He didn't want to turn, didn't want to see her face, didn't want to check out that sexy body. He couldn't afford any temptation.

"I won't be in the office Monday."

"Where will you be?" Kent halted. He wasn't aware that she'd be going somewhere.

"New York City."

"Ah, the big meeting."

"Grace did mention that I'd better get in front of the general managers, sooner than planned."

"How do you feel?" He continued walking with Dana at his side.

"Honestly?" She shrugged. "A bit petrified."

He hailed a cab and slid into the backseat.

She lowered her body to peer through the window. "So, we'll meet up when I return."

Kent lowered the window. "Dana, I will be accompanying you."

"Unnecessary." Her perfectly shaped eyebrows descended to match the icy drop in her tone.

"Such is life."

"Temporarily." She glowered at him.

Whether Dana was smiling, serious, or vexed to the max, Kent found he liked all her expressions.

"And that's a shame." He tapped the headrest to let the driver know to take off. It was good timing, too, because he turned in time to see Dana making animated gestures that didn't seem to be wishing him a good night.

10:55 p.m.
11:04 p.m.
12:50 a.m.

Kent swore aloud in the dark hotel room. He most certainly was not having a good night.

He blamed Dana for putting a curse on him. All night long, he'd tossed and turned under the comforter, on top of it, until he gave up and turned on the TV. Bored with the late-night offerings, he switched it off and tried to count sheep. Any solution that might wipe clean Dana's sexy image from his mind was fair game.

The bottom line was this: Dana Meadows wouldn't stay out of his thoughts.

Kent hugged the pillow against his body and buried his face in its softness. Just for an instant, he wanted to mimic that action with her instead. He longed to hold her against him, his body spooning hers with his face resting on her back, close to her beautiful neck. He'd feel her heart beat with his chest pressed to hers. Her voice—which wasn't deep, but rich, vibrant, and, to his English ears, had a slight drawl—carried its own power to affect his emotions.

With Dana in his arms, he'd go on a hunt for every pulse point where she'd dab her enticing perfume. He'd track their locations—behind her ear, along her neck, between her breasts, on her wrist, maybe behind her knee—and mark those spots with feathery kisses, claiming them all greedily.

Kent groaned. Desire was an eager beast that ached for satisfaction. All he could do tonight was to cup his arousal, pray for sleep and just in case, go back to counting sheep.

Kent's ideal way to wake up was by having a cup of hot black coffee, not by receiving a phone call at the crack of dawn on a Saturday from Grace Meadows. He hoped that she didn't have a grandmotherly sixth sense about his scandalous pining for Dana. Just in case, Kent pulled the comforter tightly around his body as he pinned the phone between his ear and shoulder. Her piercing voice sent any remnants of sleep skittering to the dark edges of his consciousness.

"Kent, why is Dana heading to New York City so soon? Was this based on your advice?"

"I was under the impression that this was your request for immediate action."

Grace snorted. "I don't make requests. What is my

granddaughter up to? I had planned to meet with her to go over my thoughts. I wanted the meeting to be sooner rather than later, but she wasn't supposed to leave this early."

"I think she wants to get a lay of the land before implementing a strategy. Is that a problem?" Kent hated to ask, but he felt he needed to. It seemed as if Dana had tried to outfox the old vixen. *Touché*.

"Did you finish your initial analysis of her? I don't want her barging in on the New York meeting unprepared. They are a different setup there. You can't come at them not knowing your stuff."

"All the surveys haven't been received. I don't see lack of preparation as an issue for your granddaughter."

"I just want to make sure that everything goes well. I would have come if I knew ahead of time."

Kent heard the disapproval in her voice. The Meadows matriarch was in full helicopter grandparent mode and looking for a place to land.

"You must be there. You must be my eyes and ears—"

"I'm not your spy, Grace."

"You're her coach."

"They are not synonyms."

"I'm not going to play with my word choice. Now, I have to tend to other business that requires my attention. Please make sure that you're there with Dana in New York."

"I did plan to accompany her." Kent resented the attitude that he was Dana's babysitter. But he'd hold back his comments until after he attended the New York City meeting. Grace did have it right—this meeting, which all the other heads of the various entities within Meadows Media would attend—was going to test Dana's mettle. Not only would Dana have to set the tone for the meeting, establishing that she was the company's next leader, but she would also deal with other possible contenders for the CEO position, which might emerge from this lot.

"Now that we have that settled, what's your impression?" Grace asked.

"About what?" Kent wanted to hang up the phone and head to the gym. A good workout would zap this stress and obliterate any side effects of sexual frustration. Kent would be able to socialize with people who wanted nothing from him.

"Mr. Fraser, don't toy with my intelligence. I need your instinctual response. Am I making the right decision by naming Dana my successor?"

"I think that you knew the answer before you brought me in the picture. I'm here to polish her up. Meaning that she had to have something there for me to work with." He pinched the bridge of his nose. "What it seems you want me to do is to convince the world that she is suitable. You want me to be a spin doctor."

"You sound offended." She laughed.

"Yes." Kent reached for the file he kept on Dana Meadows. The princess of a powerful family was about to have the weight of her grandmother's legacy lowered onto her shoulders in two months. His thumb traced the outline of her face in a photograph. Strong. Determined. Yet he had noticed a vulnerable quality about her when it came to her family. He wanted to know more about the inner circle of the Meadows family. In order for him to tread on such sacred land, he had to gain Dana's trust.

"Kent?"

"Yes, Grace."

"You can do this."

Kent shook his head. This woman was unbelievable. Insufferable. But she had the magic touch when it came to business. He might disagree with Grace's methods and process, but she knew how to get what she wanted.

"Toughen her up. By any means necessary," Grace instructed him.

"She's not going to war."

"If you believe that, you are just as gullible as she is. Are you, Kent?"

Kent would describe himself as many things, but gullible wasn't one. He drank a shot of cynicism every day with breakfast and visited the land of melancholia too often for his own good.

"Don't disappoint me. I'm not used to being wrong."

"Grace, when I take on a job, I give it my all. I don't set out with the idea that I *can't* help. But I'm not one of your soldiers. I have to do things my way. That means you need to step back, but also give Dana and me some room."

There was a long pause.

"Do I detect a protective tone whenever you speak about my granddaughter? My gosh! This is priceless."

Kent wished he could retract his words, or vibes, or whatever he'd tossed out there for Grace to sniff. He pulled the comforter even tighter around his body

"I should have guessed earlier. I won't stand in the way of your mild flirtation," Grace told him. "Two handsome people in a room are bound to give each other the eye. You get what you want. I get what I want." She cleared her throat. "Shocking, I know. I'm not one hundred percent barracuda."

Kent ended the incriminating conversation and hung up, not quite believing Grace's self-diagnosis He also didn't want to lend credence that she had sanctioned his approaching Dana on a personal level. To use his lust for Dana to gain her trust reeked of underhandedness. Not his style.

But then what should he do? His desire for Dana wasn't about to be put in a box marked "good behavior," no matter how how hard he tried. The longer Kent was around her, the more he learned about her, the more he interacted with her, well, the more he wanted her.

Regardless of his lust, it looked like New York City awaited him.

Kent decided to take advantage of the hotel gym, spending much longer than he normally did sweating and pounding his muscles with an hour's jog on the treadmill. When he was physically spent, Kent left the gym just as he had entered—with Dana on his mind. Back in his room, he stepped into the bathtub, turned on the showerhead, and subjected his body to the cold water. It was time for home-grown solutions to shock his libido into retreat.

Chapter 6

New York City greeted Kent with a heady mix of congestion, pungent smells of many kinds of food, and thunderous mixtures of sounds from ongoing building and street construction, harried drivers leaning on their horns, and exuberant tourists exclaiming over the city's attractions. As a world traveler, he was used to big metropolises that drew in people who wanted to turn their dreams into reality. But New York couldn't be classified with the rest. With a unique quality born of its history and diverse population, it edged out the competition.

Although he arrived a day later than Dana, he suspected that she needed the space to prepare for the next morning's meeting. Taking the opportunity to explore, he popped into a nearby coffee shop and took a seat. Once more, he opened her hometown newspaper's business section. On the front page, an article reported that Dana was leaving the "protected castle" of Meadows Media to step out into the big world to attend an important pre-board meeting. The paper didn't hold back its skepticism about a smooth transition within the ranks and clearly mocked any attempts Dana might make to lead the company.

The dated photo of Dana in the article was unflattering. It showed her emerging from a nightclub, locked arm-in-arm with a man on either side of her, flashing a wide smile. It underscored the pithy comments written in the column. Part of any battle lay in perception. This photo was a far cry from what he knew of Dana. Her public image was another item that would need readjustment.

His cell phone rang.

"Hey." It was Dana's voice. "Where are you?"

"Taking a stroll." By then, Kent had left the coffee shop and was trying to read the street signs, walk and dodge the pedestrians at the same time. "I'm heading toward Times Square." Manic flashes of light displaying ads for Broadway shows and moving images on electronic billboards guided him across the busy street. "Did you need something?"

"I was going to stretch my legs."

"Great. We could grab a meal," Kent invited.

"Wonderful. Meet you in front of the Marriott."

Kent finished up the call and hastened toward his destination. His hurried footsteps propelled him toward the woman who had overtaken his thoughts. They'd be able to talk strategy for the meeting. He had it all worked out. He could share his perspective. She could share her talking points. As Kent rounded the corner, his brisk walk turned into a light jog. He couldn't look cool and in control even if he tried.

Up ahead, he spotted Dana before she noticed his approach. She stood, cell phone at her ear, under a lit canopy. Its tiny overhead lights bathed her in a halo of bright white. Tonight's wardrobe was a black sleeveless dress that boldly clung to her shapely figure. As she turned and unintentionally posed with hip jutted, he had to admit that the back view was slightly ahead of the front view. How could he not go for her curved behind? It had just enough meat for him to hang on to.

He paused in admiring. *What if she had a date?* He hoped that she wasn't catching up with a special someone on the phone or making plans for later.

She faced him and waved. Heaven help his blood pressure. Her face lit up with a smile that touched Kent, since it was all for him.

"Beautiful evening, isn't it?" Not the most suave line, but greeting her with how she looked smashingly and downright sexy would be wrong...even if it felt so right.

"Pretty warm night." She tucked the phone in her small black purse.

"You're not still working?" He asked, hoping for some illumination as to who had been on the other end of that phone call

"Ah...no." She shook her head.

"Have you thought about where you'd like to go for dinner?" Kent asked.

She shook her head. "I'm good to go for whatever you have in mind."

He stood at the curb and tried to hail a cab, but found it difficult, since many passengers were heading to the theater that time of evening. He looked out at the heavy flow of occupied taxis.

"Forget the cabs. Let's take the subway." Dana pulled his arm to get his attention.

He didn't object to a bit of adventure with her, though boarding the train almost got them mowed over by theatergoers, tourists and the few locals who liked spending time under the evening lights of Times Square. Standing on the train like a sardine wasn't his style, except that it brought Dana closer than any other situation might have.

"Where are we going?" Kent asked. He didn't know where the train they had boarded was bound. "Greenwich Village."

"Because?" He'd never heard of the place.

Dana shrugged. "Why not?"

"I'm along for the ride." Kent meant that in every sense. He dipped his head toward hers. Her hair brushed against his nose, and the scent of apples, crisp, sweet, fresh, tantalized him.

The train jerked to a stop. Kent's body swayed and bucked to the motion in synchronized fashion with hers. They both held on to the metal bars overhead, while her back connected with his chest. His hand shot out to steady her. Its landing site on her hip wasn't planned, but not unpleasant.

"Coppin' a feel?" Dana looked up him, grinning as his face warmed.

"Just trying to be a hero. Saving you from flying across the train and cracking your skull in the process."

"Wow. Now, I hadn't seen that scenario. Guess I should count myself lucky." She faced him with a wide grin. Her nose was near his chin and her breath had a touch of mint that he would have loved to taste.

The train resumed motion again, causing his chin to brush against her downy soft hair. His fingers twitched in anticipation of tracing her hairline and disappearing into its thick silkiness.

Thank goodness for the train, which sounded like it was on its last brakes. Another screeching halt pushed his body against Dana's. Her back pressed against the train's wall and her hands shot out and gripped his shirt, bunching it at his chest. His lips smeared an arc along her forehead.

"My apologies," he lied.

"Rough ride."

"Should be over soon." His body hoped it wasn't.

"I'm not in a hurry."

He prayed that his arousal wouldn't make its own response, revealing to Dana a little more than he wanted. The only way to avoid an embarrassing moment would be to step away, break contact.

"We're here." She squinted to read the station name.

Why couldn't the train break down? Kent wished.

The train dutifully pulled into West Fourth Street station. They exited with the flow and headed up to the street level. Unlike Times Square's trademark bright lights and constant activity, the area was darker and several degrees more subdued, still busy with foot traffic, and featuring an overabundance of restaurants on either side of the avenue, and along narrow side streets.

Dana paused in front of a few establishments. "Feel like Italian? Greek? Irish?"

Kent listened to all the various ethnic options. What she didn't know was that he'd forego any of it for hotel fare in either her or his hotel room. His stomach rumbled. "Italian works for me."

They headed to a small, Italian, family-style restaurant. Seating was tightly packed along one side of the narrow building. Because it was a popular time for dining, they were seated in a rear corner. Kent had no complaints.

"Looks like we made a great pick," he said.

"Seems that way."

Their meals arrived within minutes after they'd ordered. No time for any awkward conversation to fill the space.

"All this traveling that you do…?"

"Yes." He sensed the lead-up to a heavy question.

"Is there someone back home impatiently waiting?"

Now, why hadn't he thought of that? Being direct. He shook his head. "And you?"

Dana shook her head. "Wouldn't you agree that this is the worst time for me to be involved with anyone? They'd be neglected. I'm sure as things pan out—speaking optimistically—he would feel ignored."

"Sometimes having someone makes the trials much easier to bear."

She shrugged. "Are you seriously going to be my life coach, too?"

"Now that would be an interesting addition to the curriculum vitae, but I'm not qualified. On that note, let's eat."

Kent didn't profess to have an expert taste for food. But this risotto, with large, oversized meatballs in a rich, savory tomato sauce, was damn good.

"Here, try the creamed garlic linguini. To die for." Dana pushed her plate toward him. Tonight, there were no frothy green drinks.

They picked at each other's food, sampling, sharing, teasing past each other's boundaries. A clash of forks, a brush of hands, a bump of the knee under the table in their tightly packed situation, all generated a sexually charged bubble around them

"Looks like we cleaned up well." Dana looked at his plate and then hers.

"Must have been hungrier than I felt."

"Interested in walking it off?"

Kent wanted to suggest that she might like to prepare for tomorrow. He didn't want it to end, though. "Let's go." Common sense won. He paid the bill.

They took the subway back to Times Square. The lateness of the hour and lack of travelers provided empty seats.

Kent waited for Dana to take a seat before he took his across the aisle. As much as he wanted to savor the feel of Dana's body against his, he couldn't promise any sort of self-control in a closely timed, repeat performance.

Frisky couples accompanying them on the ride didn't have the same restrictions. Kent looked out the window to avoid the passionate interludes. The reflection of a particular couple kissing as if their lives depended on it played out before him like a hot romantic movie scene. All he could do was close his eyes for his own version.

Dana immediately filled his thoughts. Her mouth partly open, soft and inviting. Those dark eyes that didn't miss anything. He squeezed his eyes tighter. His jaw clenched. Fingers curled into his palms. He wanted her so damned bad.

Dana slid into the seat next to Kent. She didn't want to think about what had stirred her to make that move.

"Look at me." No matter the cause, the effect landed her next to his warm body. "Please?" She'd beg, if she had to.

Right now, here under the glaring bright lights, on a rumbling train, she wanted more than a taste of a wild ride.

Kent turned his handsome face toward her. It was all she needed. Taking a deep breath, she mounted his lap. Her hands anchored his face. She gazed into those beautiful eyes.

"Kiss me?" Her question hung softly in the air, begging for his assent.

His gaze shifted to her mouth. Under her fingers, she felt his chin lift toward her face.

The kiss, the first contact, was soft, tentative, an introduction of sorts to each other's lips. She wrenched her mouth away from contact with his. Logic wanted to intrude. Her breathing drew heavily from her chest, as if she'd hit the treadmill for a challenging mile on an incline.

His lips, however, didn't follow her reluctance and landed softly on the rise of her breast, just above the neckline of her dress.

She arched back. An alarming jolt electrified her senses as his tongue scorched her flesh. Dana moaned her surrender before clamping her mouth on his to gag herself.

Pressed together, their lips formed an *X*, sending and receiving erotically coded messages to every part of their bodies. She welcomed his tongue's exploration of her mouth, guiding it along with sweeping forays of her own. Occasionally, she broke off contact to catch her breath. Her mouth opened to suck in air before it embraced his.

Kent's hands gripped her backside, massaging along the fleshy cheeks up to her waist. Dana's skin shivered as his hands slid up her back until he trailed his fingers into her hair. Her scalp tingled from his touch. She practically wanted to jump out of her skin as his hands continued to explore her body.

"I think we've missed our stop," she whispered against his cheek. The scent of his cologne enticed with its addictive woodsy notes, which were definitely crafted to make a female wet with sexual need.

Kent kissed her forehead as his hands slowly eased off her body.

As Dana felt him withdraw from her, she realized she didn't want it to be over. Not yet.

Slowly, she slid off him. The fact some people had been watching them didn't matter. Her pulse was revved so high that she didn't care about their reactions. All she could think about was when she could get another hit, another chance, to play at that dangerous edge of fulfillment.

Their ardor cooled as they walked out of the station

and hailed a cab. Once inside, Kent sat far away from her. He hadn't said much since they got out of the subway. She dearly wanted to have those strong hands take hold of her, his mouth to claim hers.

One sideway glance told her that the moment was gone.

They arrived at her hotel first. Dana paused as she got out. Even though she knew she didn't have any supernatural powers, she willed any mental telepathy she might possess to be activated so Kent could read her mind. She'd love to have him escort her to the door, flirt with her, ask for a nightcap, push rules aside to share her bed that night.

"Nice dinner. It's back to work. See you tomorrow," he said, his face partly turned away from her, as if he had already gotten bored.

She wasn't imagining things. He had been into her. No one kissed and responded like that if there wasn't a connection. All she wanted was that spark to ignite and let desire blaze hot and bright. Not too much to ask. Instead, Kent retreated behind a stiff upper lip like a light switch flipped to the "off" setting.

"Yeah." She picked up her pride from where it had fallen.

He moved to slide out of the car with her. "One sec," he said to the taxi driver.

"No need. I'm a big girl." Dana firmly closed the car door and walked into the hotel.

Tomorrow would definitely be a new day. She'd scrub her memory clean of Kent and continue onward. So, he wanted it to be strictly business. Nothing personal.

Chapter 7

"I don't need Kent anymore." Dana tried to dampen her desperation on the call with her grandmother the next morning before the meeting.

"What's the problem? You haven't gone to the leadership retreat yet. You haven't received his recommendations for how you can improve your business acumen."

"I know."

"You're not CEO, as of yet."

"And should I be? Grandma, should I try to follow in your footsteps? So far, it's been hard. So far, I don't… know…." Dana bit her lip to stave off crumbling into a million pieces. She couldn't tell her grandmother the true causes of her distress—the pressure to succeed and her strong attraction to Kent, all while wondering if she could push pause on life to deal with both. Kent's rebuff had stung.

The last time Dana had cried in front of her grandmother was when her mother promised to come home for Christmas. Elaine's long absence had been cloaked in whispers and adult-talk. Dana had never been allowed to know everything, the things that she only discovered later, like the fact that her mother had wandered off in full rebel mode to discover herself and emerge from Grace's shadow. A few letters overflowing with poetry and feelings, a spattering of photos of her mom posing with groups of like-minded rebels, and the two phone calls promising that she'd be home for Thanksgiving were all Dana had received. When those didn't happen, the next phone call was her promising a homecoming at Christmas.

When Dana awoke that Christmas Day, she ignored the presents and went on the hunt for her mother. But there was no sign of her. Dana had cried that day, from the first hint of the sun breaking through the horizon to its evening ritual of descent into darkness. Nothing could console her. But by the early hours of the next morning, she vowed that she would not shed another tear over heartbreak. Crying didn't change outcomes. She'd not mend her heart, just for anyone to rip it apart.

"Dana, I know you might feel overwhelmed. I guess it doesn't help that I've turned up the dial to get things in place."

"Whatever you need, Grace." Dana couldn't wait for the next two months to be done.

"You sound sad, my dear. Look, after this meeting, I want you to come home. Don't head off anywhere."

"Okay."

"By the way, your mom has been asking about you. She's at your place. Arrived this morning."

"I'll catch up with her later." Dana had gotten used to her mother popping in for brief visits.

"By the way, I'm having a small dinner party at the house in a few weeks."

Dana didn't answer. Of course, she was expected to attend.

"I'm inviting Kent, too."

"To a party? Seems like a bit much for a consultant."

"I consider him more than a consultant. He is not the enemy," Grace chided.

"But he's not a friend." Dana tried to disguise any disappointment at that fact.

"I promised to introduce him to some of my business associates. It'll be the perfect setting."

"Basically, he's in this for more than just working with Meadows Media."

"Is that what you think? My dear, you couldn't find a more dedicated man."

"Grandma, do you have the hots for him?" Dana bit her lip to keep from snorting.

"If you were here, I would smack your ears. I'm a married woman." She huffed. "I'm doing this for you."

"And the company."

"Yes, I'm interested in shoring up the longevity of Meadows Media. I am biased. When this company was just at its proposal stage, no one supported me except your grandfather. From the first to the last division I created, I've had naysayers—I was too young, the wrong gender, wrong color, the wrong everything. I jumped hurdles and knocked on and knocked down doors. So I'm not going to back down from what I want for the company."

Dana felt her grandmother's anger unleash. She'd royally pissed off the old lady and now she was about to get a tongue-lashing for her disrespect. Although her delivery could have been better, Dana had said what was on her mind. Plus, she wasn't directly face-to-face with Grace, which allowed her to be bolder in her comments.

"Don't go radio silent on me," Grace snapped. "Meadows Media carved out a niche and stayed on top of the rest. It built this house. It was, and still is, the center of this family. And I want that legacy to continue. You are the only person in the family capable of taking up the baton."

Dana felt relief for the rare compliment, as well as the familiar gush of fear. *Capable* was a weighty word.

"It is Kent's job to make sure of that."

"Yes, ma'am."

"Stop fighting him."

"I wasn't—"

"We've got a clock ticking toward the formal transition."

"And I have Peter O'Brien on my heels with his coup-like action."

"He's harmless. Take the time to win him over. He can be your greatest asset."

Dana had her own opinion of O'Brien.

"As you know, ten years ago, I retained fifty-one percent ownership, after distributing the rest. The Meadows family is the other major stockholder, with employees and private investors having a small percentage. The key now is for the family to collectively hold on to its stock. No small feat among the lot of you. But there are a bunch of stockholders that are restless and waiting to see if you've got the fortitude to keep this massive ship afloat and sailing into uncharted waters. Some young shark might be able to take the reins, but they will have no history, no love for what is here. Maybe I'm getting sentimental in my old age, but…"

Dana heard the anguish in her grandmother's voice. In that small hiccup of emotion, she heard a love that ran deep.

"It's up to you, Dana."

"Okay."

"You've got to believe it. You've got to trust."

"Okay," she reiterated with more emphasis. She didn't know how to fall in love and let it consume her. It had never happened with a man, much less with a thing—like a company.

How had her grandmother done it? Yes, she mentioned her grandfather being at her side, but the untenable attitude of the woman who had raised her couldn't be denied. The family had been born and raised around the company's growing pains and massive success.

That traditional family descent into acrimonious relationships had drifted downward to her cousins. Everyone tolerated each other under Grace's watchful eye, but only barely. Outside of the gates of the Meadows family estate, all bets were off. Grace didn't see a lot of her family, except on holidays, when stock dividends were distributed at Christmas dinner. There they would hold hands, pray and express well-wishes to one other. No one, not even Grace, was fooled by her family's contrite manner. Dana felt sure that contentious vacuum had propelled Grace into a desperate act of selecting an heir apparent, in which the grandchild she had raised was the easy fruit dangling within reach. Thus, she chose Dana for this job.

"I must say that I'm worried that you're not getting along with Kent. Maybe I should have a word with him."

"No!"

"Well, what is it, Dana?" Her grandmother's irritation resurfaced. "Obviously, he's doing something wrong if you are ready to kick him to the curb. I'm confident that he can complete his job. If he needs to soften his approach or try a new method, then he needs to know."

"It's not that I don't think he could do the job. I...I

thought that…maybe…he could leave some reading materials and I'll study them."

Grace laughed. Her grandfather called it his darling's sweet whiskey laugh. The sound had the tone of a drunken woman noisily letting everyone know how inebriated she was. Dana wasn't sure about the *sweet* part.

"I'm sure it would be cheaper to use the coaching manual and call him, if necessary." This option would most certainly cool off the mega flare-up of her carnally lustful appetite. Right now, if she continued to think of Kent as just a piece of ass, then Dana didn't have to inspect the way her heart pumped harder when she thought of him, or how her palms grew sweaty, or that she had to force herself to utter a coherent thought. Jumping Kent's bones on the train was a complete mind-to-body malfunction on her part. Never mind that, instead of pushing her aside, he joined in as if it was a game of Simon Says. Dana blamed the public display of affection on the other couples on the subway that had been romantically intertwined. They'd shot off their hormonal romantic nets to ensnare unwary bystanders like her who would never have acted on the urge otherwise.

Her embarrassment had no limits as she thought of how Kent had barely looked at her when they got back to the hotel. She could sense the tick marks on his survey about her leadership skills:

Leadership Skill: 0

Floozy: 10 points

Dana snapped back to the sound of her grandmother's voice. "Sweetheart, this isn't an online course that you pass after a certain number of weeks. This is boot-camp training for the big fight. And I'm sure there will be one. I want you prepared and ready to outthink those who smell blood in the water."

Dana often thought her grandmother relished drama in any situation. Now, she was acting as if she was a retiring general, training her successor to lead an army. Having that cutthroat mind-set didn't come naturally to Dana, but she'd try to cultivate it to win Grace's approval.

"And I'll see you at the house. Now, go handle your business and report back. Goodbye, dear."

Dana hung up. She was the first to admit that her grandmother was intense—sometimes beyond the scope of common sense.

She poured herself a cup of bold, dark coffee, mainly to warm up her fingers. In an hour, she would be addressing the general managers of the Meadows divisions. She relied on the caffeine to get her juices flowing and to kick out any lethargy. Her mind already worked on the key approach she'd use to garner unanimous support for her vision.

Though Dana relied on continuing many of Grace's plans to maintain the status quo, some were old-fashioned. Before she had interned and worked her way through Meadows, she'd also completed a summer study abroad program during her graduate studies with short stints at various corporations. While working under various management styles, she'd encountered mavericks who walked the fine lines of what was acceptable in business, who took monumental risks, who weren't afraid of failing.

What Dana most feared wasn't necessarily a coup within the business. If anything, she'd come to expect one. What had kept her up at night lately was the fear that, when she shared her latest plan with Grace, her grandmother would send her packing—not only from the company, but possibly her life.

Time to head for the next test. Dana drained her cup, then she stepped in front of the mirror to adjust her clothing. Her bangs brushed against her eyebrows and her hair hung to her shoulders in loose curls. Her stylist and her team had arrived early to get her ready. This wasn't the time to show any signs of weakness. If it meant shaping the perception of her future employees, then she'd do that. O'Brien's behavior had taught her that much.

Kent looked at the clock. As a spectator seated on the outer ring of the conference room, he likened the experience to watching a Shakespearean intrigue. The meeting was heading into its fourth hour. Food had been brought in, but no one had taken any real breaks to eat. From the intense discussion taking place, food was the last thing on the executives' minds. If he read the mood correctly, some were out for blood. A few seemed to be reserving judgment. Those who might become her supporters weren't confident enough to let their peers know which way the wind blew.

Dana didn't appear affected by the atmosphere. From her meeting with the division heads to now, she had assumed an air of confidence, or maybe it was defiance. Her new no-nonsense demeanor included him in its net.

But it was more than that. Her greeting had been frosty. When he'd tried to have a conversation, she dismissively cut it short and walked away. He didn't like it one bit.

He'd been an idiot for not acting upon her implied invitation. But he didn't operate on impulse. He preferred contemplation. Weighing the pros and cons. His style was to take it slow.

At the business level, he was excellent at information retrieval, the processing and synthesizing of information. He treated his relationships as if they were his business techniques. So far, it worked for him. Risk-free. Low tolerance of failure.

"We'll take a break." Dana picked up the meeting

agenda and flipped through it. "We'll meet back here at three o'clock." Without waiting for any response, she exited the room.

Kent grabbed his materials and chased after her. He didn't say anything until he caught up. "What's the problem?"

"What?" She looked exasperated, but kept moving.

"Why are you on the run?"

"Although we have a break, I still have work to complete," she answered.

"Up for lunch?"

She shook her head. "I have reports to read."

"I need to eat."

"Then go do that." She pushed past him. "Now, if you'll excuse me."

"I wasn't done talking." Kent followed her toward the elevator.

"Well, I'm done listening."

The elevator doors opened and he swore that she increased her speed into the cab that was depositing noisy tourists into the lobby. She turned and pressed the Door Close button. Her cool smile said it all.

He ran and placed his arm between the doors, willing to let them slam it if it would impede her retreat.

"What do you want, Kent?" As he boarded the elevator, she stepped to the corner of the cab that was farthest away from him.

"You're angry."

"Aren't you the smart one?" She pushed the button again. "Which floor?"

"I'm going to your room."

"No, you're not." She crossed her arms, eyes blazing.

The doors opened on her floor. She stepped out, but she pushed him back into the cab.

"Whatever I did, I'm sorry," Kent offered.

"Maybe it's what you didn't do."

The doors shut and the elevator rose. Kent pushed the button to send the elevator back down to Dana's floor.

He stepped onto the floor just as she was entering her room. "Dana, wait." He knew better than to wait for her to acknowledge him, so he ran down the hallway and pounded on her door. "Dana, please open up."

Kent couldn't stop kicking himself for not going after Dana last night. His conscience, the moral high ground, his professional code of ethics had derailed the impulse to follow through with what naturally had arisen.

More than physical attraction kept him pounding on the door. More than his job to coach a new leader had him ready to cross the professional line. He recognized a kindred spirit who was independent, risk-taking and bold. And yet, her compassion, thoughtfulness and sense of duty spoke his personal language. They could fit together like perfect puzzle pieces, if only he hadn't screwed up.

From other rooms, heads emerged at his loud appeal. But the one person he wanted to talk to didn't respond. After a few minutes, he gave up knocking. "What didn't I do, Dana?" he said softly.

The door swung open and he almost fell in. "You didn't man up to your feelings. I know something sparked between us. I felt it." She brushed his hand from where it had come to rest on her shoulder. "You acted like nothing happened."

"I acted like someone who wanted to keep his job." Kent raised her chin with a finger and looked deeply into her eyes. "I acted like someone who didn't want to be mistaken for someone who acts disrespectfully with his client." He sighed. "I behaved like a coward."

Dana pulled him toward her. "Even the Cowardly Lion

was cute." She pinched the air with her fingers to indicate a small amount. "A little bit." She planted a tantalizingly wet kiss on his mouth, then asked, "Why are you here, Kent?"

"I want to finish what we started."

"Really? You want a one-time quickie so you can write 'Task Accomplished' on my evaluation?" She squinted at him. "You didn't strike me as the type."

"You don't want a relationship?"

"No. But I'm intrigued enough to play along."

Kent had never had such a casual arrangement thrust upon him. He remembered the feel of Dana in his hands, on his lap, against his hips. Even now, his body and mind became aroused together. "Again, why are you here, Kent?" Dana leaned in to the point where the tips of their noses touched. "Don't step into the ring if you're not willing to play the game." A soft kiss brushed his cheek.

"No rules?"

"We'll make them up as we go along." She started unbuttoning his shirt.

"Grace?"

"She's not invited."

Kent laughed. The hilarity diminished as Dana deposited a series of small kisses along the path from his cheek to his ear. Her tongue bathed the coil of his ear, tickling and inciting spastic muscle responses.

He held her, still meaning to break contact. "This doesn't mean that I'm going to roll over on my job."

She blew in his ear before nipping at his earlobe.

"I may have to be firm."

She cupped his crotch and softly squeezed. "I'd say you're all the way there."

Kent rested his forehead against the top of her head. Suddenly, his breath hitched as if he'd run a mile in five minutes. His pulse ratcheted several beats up the pressure gauge. She wouldn't stop kneading his crotch and kissing the nape of his neck.

"I've never been tempted like this," he croaked.

"That's good. Wouldn't want you to be an easy lay," she teased

"I'm feeling like the sensitive one." Her hot kisses had him ready to spout gibberish.

Dana covered his mouth with hers and he accepted her invitation to lead this dance. His tongue swept over hers, stroking as he pulled his shirt off and tossed it to the side. He craved the feel of her soft skin sliding against his.

She matched his movements, undressing from the top down. Each layer of clothing removed revealed more smooth brown skin. Once naked, she had the body and feminine grace of an earthly goddess, all of which supercharged his feelings from longing into rabid need.

As Kent picked her up by her hips and carried her to the bed, she wrapped her legs around him, her breasts pressed against his chest. Her arms wound around his neck as she arched herself back, offering herself up to him. Never one to refuse a delicious treat, he kissed and sucked on her neck.

"Don't you dare leave me with a hickey."

He laughed at the visual of her heading back to the meeting in the afternoon with a deep red, telltale bruise. "You taste so good," he moaned. He halted momentarily and laid her on the bed, his torso still trapped between her legs.

"My pocketbook. I have condoms." She addressed his pause. "Always prepared for the unexpected. Safety first."

He retrieved the protection and slid it on himself. "Ready?"

"Since last night."

Kent sat back to survey the beautiful landscape spread

out before him. The long, shapely legs opened in an in-
verted V on either side of him. At their apex, he admired
the trimmed curls, under which lay moist inner trappings
he just *had* to taste before diving in. But there were other
parts to explore first. With reluctance, he tore his gaze
from her mound up to her flat stomach. His fingers didn't
want to be left. As his fingertips touched her skin, and she
twitched, he followed the lines of her ribs, running over
their ridges toward the swell of her breasts.

Now, his mouth took over, latching over the tight bud of
her nipple. He sucked, pulling and teasing with his tongue.
Her moans grew labored and guttural.

"Now…" Her pelvis bucked for his attention.

"Stop calling the shots." A long kiss from him quieted
her protests. Her mouth was pure honey that he couldn't
get enough of. Dana's arms tightened around him, her nails
pressing into his back. As pain mixed with pleasure, his
own grunts intermingled with her soulful moans.

She had no idea how much he stood on the edge of an
orgasm, without even entering her. The momentum to fall
and succumb to whatever fate had in mind pushed past
the last strands of reason that he held on to. As he licked
her body from north to south, he surrendered to the call.

He wanted to touch her everywhere. His lips did the
work. Heading due south, he dived in between her legs and
buried his tongue in her. Her juices bathed his tongue like
a honeyed trail. He kissed outer and inner labia, branding
them with his kisses. He learned every inch of her body,
committing it to memory. Already, he told himself that it
was all only temporary.

Her engorged clit suffered under his onslaught. He made
no apologies for the rough attention. His tongue painted her
with fierce brushstrokes and swirls around her opening.

"You can't make me wait." She grabbed his head.

"Bossy woman." His accusation came out muffled as he fluttered her clit with his tongue. More juice flowed, wetting his lips further.

He heeded her body's signals. Slowly he entered, sliding along her lubricated walls that hugged his shaft.

Her hips tilted up, coaxing him to reach farther, deeper into her. Her eyes were closed. She bit her bottom lip. Her hands slid up his chest. Fingers curled over his pecs, pressing into his flesh.

"Harder," she demanded between gritted teeth. She twisted his nipples and clawed at him. "Oh...harder."

Kent never had a problem following directions. Now was no different. He pumped hard, like his life depended on it. Her walls answered with their quivering response. His hands were occupied with pinning her to the bed, holding her wrists above her head. Desire rolled over him like the incoming tide, one wave folding into another, building with frequency and intensity. His butt clenched as his climax built.

"I can't hold on." Her body almost lifted off the bed, arced as if in pain.

Kent didn't mean for Dana to be deprived of more pleasure. He reared back on his haunches, lifting Dana onto his hips. He gave her the ride of her life.

With her arm wrapped around his shoulder, she held on as if she was riding a mechanical bull. Her head and arm whipped back and forth. Every movement, no matter how slight, rubbed the tip of his shaft tantalizingly.

Now it was his turn to savor the muscles moving under his fingers. He raised her off his hips and brought her down, repeatedly pounding into her. Her mouth opening into a soundless O turned him on to a point even higher than where he was before.

There. That twitch of her hips unhinged him. No longer

able to hold back, he released himself. She didn't penny pinch on her reaction, either.

It was as if they jumped off a cliff without a parachute, soaring, flying, floating on a current that was in tune with their vibrations. It didn't matter if one came first because hand-in-hand, each climaxed with a ferocity that only Mother Nature could create.

Chapter 8

"Ready to face the world?"

"Wish I didn't have to." Dana snuggled deeper in the crook of Kent's arm, where she had rested for the past hour. She wanted to stay in the afterglow of their fantastic sexual interlude. But the longer they stayed in bed, the more likely they'd have to talk and rationalize their behavior. And she didn't want to face consequences or reason her way through her impulsive need to sleep with Kent. He hadn't wanted her that way last night. Today, he didn't disappoint. Why? She wasn't that beguiling.

"You know, you've only got forty minutes before you head back into the meeting."

"Guess I need to get on my game face."

"I'm not complaining."

"Well, you might when you hear what I have to say." Her decision solidified as soon as her heart rate returned to normal. That time allowed for her to separate emotional reaction from necessity.

He didn't respond right away. "Talk to me."

"The second half of the meeting will be highly confidential. I know you've signed an agreement, but we're heading into territory that's beyond your...clearance—so to speak."

Kent didn't respond. He didn't have to. She felt his body stiffen next to her and, this time, it wasn't about sexual urge.

"Let me explain." She resisted kissing his flattened nipple, though her tongue so wanted to trace the circle. She balled her fist and kept her hand tightly against her body, instead of reaching for him and enjoying the way his arousal was currently transforming into a rigid rod.

"No, it's okay," he said. "It's your family's company and it's not as if I can't do my job without being your shadow. As things go, I do have to make a trip back to England."

She turned over onto her stomach and propped her chin on his chest. "For how long?" That whining voice. Gosh, she didn't mean to sound wanting. But England was more than a few hundred miles to the next state. Distance didn't bode well for relationships, no matter how sincere the desire of the couple. Her mother's moving from India to Jamaica to Europe, while Dana stayed with Grace, proved that point.

"I'll be gone for a week, maybe two. Not long. Some legal work has to be completed so I can begin opening an office here."

"You're serious about conquering the U.S." Now she had hope ringing clear in her voice. Kent nodded with a wide grin. "Did you get your invite from Grace?"

He shook his head.

"She's hosting a command performance at the house. I'm sure she expects you to be there."

"The Meadows women, once again bossing someone."

"Look, I didn't say you have to be there. Nor am I expecting you to do anything for me…after this." His criticism stung.

"I didn't say it was a bad thing."

"You're not making it sound like it's a good thing, either." She held his chin and fixed him with a stare. "I'm not the kind of person to make you feel like you've got to hang on. I'm a grown woman."

"You don't let the dust settle, do you? Always ready to do battle and then investigate the aftermath."

"You talk funny." She pulled away and sat with her back to him. Receiving a diagnosis didn't sit well with her. She pulled the top sheet around her shoulders as her gaze spanned the room, but she saw nothing. Too many wishes filled her mind with what-if scenarios. She turned her head, but didn't look at him.

What if her feelings were one-sided? She slid off the bed and reached for her underwear. Not since her college days had she felt this pliable and emotional. Not since then had she wanted to believe in a future, in what might come on the day after. Trust was hard to bank on, hard to hold on to, a tiny grain with so much impact that often slipped through her fingers. If she turned and looked at him, right now, she would crumple and believe.

"I'm not going anywhere, Dana." His declaration shot down any of the objections that she was lining up, ready to fire. Having men drape themselves around her because of her family name was a frequent occurrence. Their presence, she admitted to herself, was as much a reflection of her life choices as it was of the men choosing her as their target.

The bed shifted under his weight as he moved closer. She felt him position himself to sit behind her. Gently, he laid her back against his chest, one hand intertwining with hers.

"I want you to stick around," Dana said.

"You sure?" He kissed the back of her head.

"I don't want to say no. I'm not entirely sure about yes." She stopped talking because to her ears, she sounded wishy-washy. "I can't help looking forward to the next minute, the next hour, the next day, with you."

"A hopeless romantic."

"No. I'm a *hopeful* romantic."

Dana wanted to float on the bubble of giddiness. He kissed her temple, and a key unlocked another wave of desire in her. This man had no idea how much she craved his touch. If she couldn't stop moaning, he'd know her weak points.

Kent turned her around to face him. As soon as her lips could reach his, she kissed him.

He gently brushed her hair off her face. His palm rested against her skin, making her feel warm and safe.

"Since you're banishing me, I must have you once more."

"No objections there." She loved the feel of his mouth, soft and firm, coaxing and speaking to her in its intimate language. No translation was necessary for what they both wanted. She kissed him and then slipped a condom onto his shaft.

This time, she lingered over each thrust, pushing against his hips, squirming to an internal beat. Together, they bonded, tight and fierce. Each wave of longing, every rustle of her senses, every smidgeon of lust—she wanted to savor them all. Until now, her life had gone by at such a frenetic speed that grinding on *her* man's hips seemed like a delightful way to spend the afternoon.

Kent planted kisses above her breasts. Her hips bucked

forward, guiding him to touch that sensitive spot deep within her cavern. She squeezed her muscles and released to suck him in further, then her cries grew louder and wild. They'd surely test the thickness of the hotel's walls.

On the edge of the bed, their bodies were locked in a writhing mass. Kent fell onto his back and she naturally fell with him. They rolled to the middle of the bed, their bodies caught up in the sheet. Then, they were sliding headfirst off the bed onto the floor.

Kent reached over her and pulled down the comforter, then lifting Dana and setting her down on it. She saw so much strength, not only in his face with its strong jawline, not only in the planes of his body's athletic build, but within his being. She placed her hand over his heart. Inside there was a calming disposition.

Right now, she wasn't looking for calm. She bit his shoulder. He bucked hard against her pelvis. Her fingers dug into his back, while her hips torqued from the hot flames of desire. For a second time, this man had taken her to new heights, like an expert guide sharing beauty and passion with her. Gladly, she accepted the invitation with more than a little fervor until her inner walls quivered, flooding the intimate space between them with her natural juices. Like a good partner, Kent answered her call with his own release. She wasn't the type to one-up someone, and, for a second time, she came. Her body didn't disappoint him, with its reaction matching his, beat for beat. Every ounce of their energy was expended.

"Mr. Fraser, it's been a pleasure."

"I look forward to doing this again." He kissed her forehead.

"Stop doing that. I have to get back to the meeting. I've already compromised quite a few brain cells thanks to that wicked mouth of yours."

"I'll try to restrain myself." He slid his mouth down her torso.

"Damn it, Kent." Dana sighed. "Not the tongue." Her eyes rolled up in her head as if she was under the influence.

After the meeting resolved satisfactorily, Dana returned home, while Kent went to England. The reports from the divisions, during the meeting, had been fairly positive. While some executives were more restrained in their support of Dana, it wasn't due to a lack of confidence in her leadership. The most confidential part of the meeting allowed them to air their concerns about the way Meadows Media would continue to be structured. Dana understood their concerns. Though she wasn't of the mindset to blindly promise anything, she could provide the necessary support and resources to continue business as usual.

Now to prepare for the board meeting.

One week passed with no word from Kent. Then the second week passed excruciatingly slowly. The only correspondence from him was the survey results he sent to her and Grace. By the third week, another work email arrived with the preliminary work needed for the business analysis. Dana was ready to bite her nails in anticipation of any note of a personal nature.

She'd called once, left a message, and waited. That was the worst. Holding on, waiting, like a sad puppy waiting to be stroked. It was the reason why she refused to make a second call or leave another message.

This unsettling position prompted her to put work aside for a brief time and to do something—anything—to shut out Kent. That's why she was in her casual clothes with a glass of wine in one hand and a box of chocolates in her lap. Her cousin, Belinda, wasn't amused with Dana's unannounced drop-in at her home or that she'd raided her stash of munchies.

"I know that I'm not always the best listener. But I am sensing that something is on your mind. I'm here if you want to talk." Belinda motioned for her to speak.

Dana had never relied on girlfriends outside of the family when she wanted to confess her private business. She had learned that the hard way, through too many wayward social media posts about her private goings-on, which made her withdraw and trust more in her cousins' advice. "I met someone."

"Yeah? Special?"

Dana nodded. "Still feeling a little raw about it."

"I won't push. So, what do you want to talk about?"

"You know we've got to talk about Grace's party." Dana was grateful for the reprieve. She bit into a piece of chocolate and inspected the caramel center.

Belinda raised her hands in protest. "I'm not on the organizing committee."

"All of the cousins are supposed to do it."

"Um…you know that's not true. Grandma wouldn't trust anyone but you with that assignment."

"I'm pretty busy with the company." Dana popped the rest of the chocolate in her mouth and licked the remnants off her fingers. Her cheek bulged as she chewed, part of her attention on her next choice.

"Stay within the dotted lines and you'll be fine."

"Stop being sarcastic." Dana chose a chocolate-covered coconut piece. Not her favorite, but when the chocolates cost as much as these and hailed from a small European country, somehow she felt it was a sacrilege not to eat every piece.

"Where do you plan to hold the party?"

"At the house, of course."

"Every function is at that house. The place might as well be turned into a state house with the amount of official visits and parties that are held there." Belinda was known for coming up with excuses not to show up to family events.

"Or we could have it here." Dana looked over the surroundings to imagine a do-over.

"Are you crazy? My horses would object."

Dana rolled her eyes. She wasn't a horse person. Belinda had grown up with animals around her and training Thoroughbreds fit in line with her career. But, more than that, Belinda had land. A few tents here and there and they could have Grace's birthday party on the grounds.

"Rent out a museum. It'll give the classy atmosphere that Grandma likes. You can have caterers and a string quartet," Belinda offered, now aware that Dana had some ulterior motive for dropping in.

"That sounds boring."

"Like I said, stay within the lines." Belinda motioned with her head toward the kitchen—and the exit—indicating Dana should follow.

"Do you think the entire family will come?"

"Probably not, but only deal with one thing at a time." Belinda waited for Dana impatiently. Her cousin was tossing—or *escorting*—her out.

"Planning Grace's party is just as hard as taking up the reins at Meadows Media," Dana said.

"Because there's the same pain in the you-know-where in the mix."

Dana stopped following Belinda. "You know that is wrong. Grandma is tough, but she had to be to raise our mothers and work at the same time."

"Oh, stop with the public service announcement. You're the favorite. You don't get to preach." Belinda had led her to the stables. Clearly, she wanted to get back to work.

Dana pondered Belinda's comments. Dana had always been considered the favorite, not that she could prevent the privilege or curse after being left at her grandmother's. The rest of her cousins had always had their mothers in their lives. In order to have had those precious moments with her mother, Dana would exchange the label as Grace's "favorite" in a minute. Now that her mother was back in her life, everyone expected that she had gotten over it. Some days, Dana thought she had. It was those lonely times when she didn't have anything to hold her attention or tax her energy that she thought about the day her mother left for five years.

In her Sunday best with shiny black shoes, hair neatly combed, Dana thought they were going on a car trip with her mother's boyfriend. She'd heard them talk about going to see some guru who was touring the country. Finding themselves was the order of the day. However, that mission didn't include an unnecessary addition—Dana.

Sitting in the backseat, barely able to see out the window, she'd watched the familiar landscape of her hometown flash by, wondering when they would get on their way. Instead, they pulled into the Symphony Woods neighborhood. Even then, wealth hung over mansions with little regard for those who didn't have much.

After a heated discussion, Dana was left with her grandparents. They were furious with their daughter who always marched to the beat of her own drum. Thankfully, they never turned their anger and frustration onto their granddaughter.

Dana snapped back to reality.

As they strolled near the stables, she remarked, "I can't do this on my own. And yes, I do want to do this right. I want all of the family to attend."

"Honey, there aren't enough days in the calendar for the amount of work that will entail."

"Grandma asked me to do this."

"I doubt that it was a question." Belinda held up her hand against Dana's objections. "I have a show in three months. There's only so much that I will be able to do. But I don't want to see you burdened."

Dana stroked the nose of a sedate pony. She wished all creatures could have this calm temperament. Grace had insisted that she learned to ride, calling it a good exercise to induce a sense of refinement. That claim was exaggerated. As a bonus, though, Dana had enjoyed riding, which gave her an escape into her own imaginary land, where she was an abducted princess rescued by a fearless knight. Only no one came to her rescue in real life. Eventually, she learned not to look for help, not to expect it, finally settling down and surrendering to her grandmother's will.

"What about Fiona? Can she help?" Belinda didn't seem to mind making suggestions, even if she didn't want to host the party.

"Oh, good grief. That'd be like waiting for the Easter Bunny to pop in during Thanksgiving."

Belinda laughed. "Our cousin isn't that bad. It's not like she'd be deliberately unreliable."

"She might as well be married to that detective job."

"Working in the Missing Persons Unit is important to her." Belinda and Fiona were closer than Dana was to their cousin. When family arguments were underway, divided loyalties could prolong the skirmishes longer than anyone wanted.

"I know. I know. I just wish that I could see her more often. 'Cause when we do, she looks so exhausted. The job is eating her alive."

"Well, well, looks like you wenches can't stop talking about me behind my back." Fiona's voice came out of nowhere.

"Fiona! We didn't expect to see you." Dana winked at Belinda and went over to hug her cousin.

"Let's go for a ride," Belinda stepped in, as usual ready to defuse any tension.

"I'm only here for an hour. Gotta get back to—"

"Work." Both Belinda and Dana filled in with the usual excuse.

"Don't give me a hard time." Fiona did look drawn and worn around the edges.

Dana still had her arm around her cousin's shoulders. "Don't mean to. We're all busy."

"Yeah." Fiona touched her forehead to Dana's. "So what's up? When you called me earlier, you said that you wanted to talk about Grandma's birthday party. Why not hire a party planner?"

"I will, but that's not the problem." Dana wished her family didn't have so much drama.

Belinda led the way back to the house. "Seems like I'm not going to get any work done today with both of you bickering. Let's go sit on the patio. Dana, I have your favorite drink made."

"I can't drink sangrias while I'm on the clock." Fiona hooked her arm through Dana's as they headed toward the back of the house. "I'll take a virgin whatever you've got."

Dana offered up one of her old excuses. "Call in sick. Tell them you ate something bad at lunch."

"Don't you need to be at work ruling the media world?"

"Yeah, but I'm also the rogue heiress who lacks discipline and stamina. Plus, I can't seem to hold on to the one man who got a hold of me." Dana felt ready to spill.

"Do tell." Fiona got comfortable.

"Wait, don't start talking." Belinda showed up with

fruity drinks in tall glasses with tiny umbrellas decorating the tops. "And stop quoting those jackasses."

Dana couldn't stop. Her constant critics, both at work and in her own family, had managed to infiltrate her brain. Their every command flooded her system. Chin up—not high enough. Shoulders back—like Grace. Dress to impress—not likely.

"Who is the bastard?" Fiona sniffed her drink before taking a sip. "This is good."

"Told you I know what I'm doing."

"Those bartending classes paid off." Dana tasted hers. "And he's British."

"Okay, a British bastard." Fiona shrugged.

"I like him," Dana defended.

"And…?" Belinda was tentative with her questions.

"He doesn't like me." Dana explained the details, trying not to color the story with too much anger.

"Doesn't sound to me like he doesn't like you," Belinda offered. "Maybe he's not the type to talk about his feelings until he's in front of you."

"Did you give up the goodies?" Fiona made a face. "He might have thought, 'Well, my coaching job is now complete. Cheerio!'"

Belinda slapped Fiona's shoulder. "You are not helping."

Dana had already thought about all the sordid scenarios. The more she mulled it over, the worse the scenarios her imagination produced became. What if he did have a girlfriend back at home? She let out a loud groan.

"Enough. Let's leave…what's his name?" Belinda asked.

"Kent."

"British bastard," Fiona repeated, moving her shoulder out of reach of Belinda's assault.

"Well, let's leave Kent on the backburner for the moment." Belinda raised her glass and the others joined in.

"To the Meadows clan and its colorful, living history. But don't get your hopes up that you'll get all of us Meadows women together."

"Especially Great-Aunt Jen. She'll come, but she's bound to make a scene." Fiona laughed.

"That's why I'll need you guys to help me." Dana clasped her hands to plead her case. "Time is precious. Grace isn't going to live forever. We need to do right by her. We need to come together and celebrate—I mean, *really* celebrate—all that she has done."

"Well, is Grace going to make amends with her daughters first? It's not a one-way street, Dana. Our mothers have their baggage from being her kids and, like we said, Great-Aunt Jen isn't feeling her sister. What the heck happened with those two, anyway?" Belinda shifted to get comfortable in her chair.

Dana didn't answer. She'd heard some tidbits of what had caused animosity between Jen and Grace. Not only had Grace become the star in the family, she had been accused of stealing Jen's fiancé. Dana found that it was hard to think of Grace as a hot, sexy mama. But if her cousins didn't know the details, she certainly wasn't putting them on the table.

"Dana? What happened?" Belinda pushed. "I hate it when you hold back on good gossip."

"That's not important. We've got to get busy with the planning."

Fiona drained her glass. "Okay, we'll drop the matter… for now." Her phone chirped its incoming message. "Ladies, I've got to go."

"We didn't get anything accomplished." Dana wished that she could toss out Fiona's constantly ringing phone.

"We never do." Belinda sounded miffed that she hadn't gotten anything juicy out of this meet-up.

"Look, I can't afford not to do this right," Dana said. "Let's meet up again. Next weekend. My place?"

"Why do you make it sound as if you really have a separate home? And then, if we do it at your place, we'll have to stop in to say hi to Grandma." Belinda was up on her feet, ready to push both cousins out the door.

"Actually, she did complain that no one visits," Dana said.

"Because you have to come dressed as if you're going to church." Fiona fixed her standard black pantsuit, white shirt, and sensible black shoes. Even her hair was worn in a classic style, pulled back in a ponytail and wound around into a bun. She wore no makeup except for her lip balm during the winter months.

"I'm always in her crosshairs to meet someone," Belinda said. "According to her, I'm like a spinster cat lady, except I have horses. Either way, I'm doomed to be a lonely woman who has let life and love pass me by."

"That sounds awful and sad." Fiona jingled her keys. She always seemed on the verge of sprinting off. "But kind of true, Belinda."

Dana snorted. Fiona did know how to be blunt.

Belinda flipped her off and stalked off toward her beloved horses.

Dana was left alone with half a glass of sangria, as Fiona headed toward her car. She pulled out her cell phone and checked for a message from Kent. Nothing.

She headed back to the patio, settled back in a chair, and continued sipping the sangria. If she was keeping a tally of things on her to-do list that she had accomplished, she had to declare her momentum akin to spinning wheels in mud. She pulled out her phone again. "I left a message," Dana said.

"This one matters?" Belinda asked.

Dana nodded. Her cousins had all heard about her dating wars. In all previous cases, she was the one to send the guy packing. Never had she lingered or second-guessed herself. When the feeling came that she needed to cut them loose, she did.

Now, Fate had seemed to intervene, turning the tables on her. She didn't like it one bit.

"Call him again. Until he says that he's not interested, you should call him."

"Sounds stalker-ish. Not my style." Dana shook her head with a definitive shake.

"Then move on. No man is worth you sitting here looking like you've got issues. It sounds like I have got to meet this dude. But you need to snap out of it." Belinda came over and hugged her. "Now let my bad-ass cousin back into her body. Meadows women don't lose their minds over any man."

Grace Meadows. The name had people falling all over themselves to impress her. Over the years, Grace had let it go to her head. Some would argue that it still fed her ego, Grace thought to herself as she stood at her bedroom window overlooking the front of the house. She preferred watching those who entered her home to just staring out at a garden of flowers. It was the way she marked time and perhaps, she considered, her influence, measured by the number of callers she received.

Visitors would be overjoyed to be invited to her home. State officials seeking donations, celebrities wanting magazine features, people from every corner of the world—all attended her charity galas. They all came to sit and smile and indulge her with their attention.

In these twilight years, the pilgrimage had diminished somewhat, Grace mused. Except that, recently, she had noticed there was a flicker of renewed interest because she'd announced her resignation from Meadows Media. Once again, the hall and great room of her home would be filled with people for her birthday.

Grace allowed the curtain to fall in place. Her heart swelled with sadness, which was seemingly never far away these days. Building up successes in her professional life left another part of her life unattended and feeling chaotic. Now it was time to put that in order. She took a seat and waited for Leona to update her.

"Mrs. Meadows, you'd inquired about Dana. She hasn't returned home yet this evening."

"But she's in the city." Grace had sent Leona to Dana's house to summon her—as usual.

"Yes. She's been to work today."

Grace had to admit that she was quite pleased with how things were falling into place. A week ago, the meeting in New York City had gone well. Dana had hit a stride that seemed comfortable for her. Grace could only hope so, because she barely saw her busy granddaughter.

Over the last few days, she'd finally reviewed the survey results. It wasn't a detailed report, but Grace expected to get that when Kent returned from England. While she wasn't aware of any problems between Kent and her grand-daugther, outside of Dana's initial hesitancy to accept him, Grace couldn't get Dana to discuss her progress with Kent. Well, when he returned, they'd both have to meet with her.

Leona continued with her daily run-through. "We're all set for the dinner party tonight. Both Dana and Kent have RSVP'd that they will be here."

"Good." If the only way she could get her answers was by commanding attendance, then that was fine. It didn't mean that they wouldn't feel her displeasure. "Any additional RSVPs?"

"No. But you did get a request from an IPO group."

"To come to my private party?"

"Yes."

Grace knew that people were sniffing like dogs in heat for a chance to cash in on her company. They didn't scare her; they just mainly were nuisances. But this dinner was to be an official coming-out party for Dana. A few stragglers, who might have their reservations about her youngest grandchild running Meadows Media, still needed to be encouraged to come. Understandable. But unacceptable.

"Where's Henry?" Grace turned her attention to more personal matters.

"He's waiting for you. Downstairs."

"The story of my life…and his. Time to head to the doctor."

"The car is out front."

"He's not going to like not being able to drive." Grace gave herself a once-over in the mirror. "Mind you, his driving makes my heart weak—and I don't mean in a romantic sense."

Leona hid her laugh by burying her chin in her chest. She quickly exited.

Grace waited until she was sure that Leona wasn't returning. Slowly, she let out a deep breath and allowed herself to show what she didn't want anyone to see—the pain etched on her face from her arthritis, a daily annoyance caused by swollen joints.

The memory blanks were a different problem, one that scared her more than she'd ever let on. She pushed up from the chair. Her hand gripped the armrest until she was steady. Only then did she move to head downstairs.

Grace pasted on a bright smile and determinedly shook off her body's gradual failings. Right now, she was off for Henry's follow-up appointment after cataract surgery. She

suspected that all would be well. Then they'd be back for
a dinner reception that would be grand enough to be written up in the local paper. Hopefully Kent had worked his
magic. Dana would be ready for the crown, and she could
rest easy about Meadows Media.

The Meadows Media file lay open on Kent's desk. He
had written his detailed report of Dana's progress thus far,
along with a few recommendations. That took care of the
work stuff. What he hadn't taken care of was matters of
the heart. And he wasn't in denial that a certain woman
stirred more than his interest. He was simply unsure as to
how to handle his emotions.

The paperwork in front of him only shed a partial light
on who she really was. In order to get to know her, he had
to put aside the facts about her educational background, her
places of employment, and her press clippings that made
her sound like Mother Teresa. Walking into unknown territory without a backup plan, as he had done, took him out
of his comfort zone.

What he wanted to know was the little things. Did she
sleep in just a T-shirt or a full pajama set? Did she prefer
perfume or her natural scent? Would she choose a lobster
dinner or filet mignon? Regardless of the answers, for there
were no right or wrong ones, he wanted to run his fingers
through her hair and pull her mouth to meet his. Every day
he wanted to taste her. His memory of their time together
was no longer enough.

He had felt terribly guilty about being M.I.A. from Dana
since he'd been in England—and for purposely extending
his stay longer than expected—but he had needed time to
collect his thoughts. Over the last two weeks, he had pondered and agonized about the possibility that, if he began
a relationship with good intentions, he might devolve into

his father. Would he destroy Dana's expectations and cause her pain? He didn't want that. He had never felt so strongly for any woman before.

"Knock. Knock."

"What are you doing here?" Kent rounded his desk and embraced Conrad, who had indeed lost his job. The immediate aftermath had not been pretty, with his binge drinking and general depression. Since he had been in America, Kent hadn't been there to support and drag him back to the land of living. Guilt weighed on his conscience, but he was happy that Conrad knew he was back and had reached out. "Came to drag you out." Conrad's expression was mischievous.

"I'm busy." Kent held up the files.

"You've avoided me since you got back. I'm tired of talking to your secretary and your voicemail." Conrad closed the files and kept his hand on them. "Plus, I have a job now. Time to hit the pub."

Kent had missed his friend. And since he had to return to America soon, he had better act on the invitation before several more weeks passed without contact. Plus a good cold beer would hit the spot. Kent surrendered and left the office with his friend.

"You know that you are a bad influence." Kent followed the after-work crowd heading to their favorite drinking spots.

"I remember doing some crazy things that you cooked up."

"And did we get caught?"

Conrad laughed. "Every bloody time."

Kent punched his arm. "We were part of the Essex Estate crew. A lot of good that did us."

"Got sent to St. Francis School for Boys." Conrad

stopped to admire a young woman strutting past. "And they almost kicked us out."

"Please stop. Your trip down memory lane is depressing."

Conrad held open the pub door. "The point is: Look how far we've come."

Kent looked at him and shook his head. "Yeah, this is a mighty big step."

The pub was one of only three they frequented. They knew the staff and some of the usual suspects who came after work.

"We've got a table."

Kent followed Conrad, wondering how he'd managed to get a table at the peak of the day.

"Surprise!" Conrad stepped aside to reveal Agatha, waiting with a glass of white wine in front of her.

"What?" Kent closed his eyes and opened them to refresh his vision. "Why?"

"You sit next to your honey and I'll sit across from you." Conrad signaled to the waitress for two more drinks. "I'll wet my whistle and then leave you lovebirds alone."

Kent didn't budge from where he stood. His friend's pride in what he'd accomplished had muddled the uncomfortable situation further.

"Hi, Kent." Agatha looked different, yet she hadn't markedly changed her physical appearance. Maybe her hair was shorter. Whatever the change, he didn't want to ponder it.

"I wasn't expecting to see you," Kent said slowly. In his mind, they had broken up and at least *he* had moved on.

"Noted." She offered a smile. "But I'm here now. Conrad was sweet enough to make it happen."

"I want to see you happy." His friend looked up at him. "You've been down in the dumps. Not talking to me. I know you all had…well, taken some time off. But we're back—the happy trio." Conrad took the beers and slid one over to Kent. "Come on, sit. We'll be here for a while."

Kent reluctantly complied. He was going to kill Conrad when they were alone. Right now, he had no desire to keep up a charade that he was interested in rekindling feelings that were never there.

"It really is good to see you." Agatha reached for his hand. He pulled it off the table, along with his feelings.

"Agatha and I held down the fort until your return." Conrad grinned at him. "I, for one, missed eating well." Kent usually picked up the tab, which he didn't mind doing.

"I'd rather not to do this in public." Kent pushed himself up from the seat.

"Please, let's talk." Agatha grabbed his wrist.

Kent looked at Conrad, his look partly pleading and partly urging his friend to fix this train wreck.

"Sweetheart, I think that I made a big mistake." Conrad attempted to break the tension. "I got over-enthusiastic with doing good deeds."

"You didn't change your mind about us?" Agatha ignored Conrad.

"No." Kent looked down at the table with its carvings that dated back to the nineties. Hearts and initials decorated the warped wood. A good number of couples had come here to celebrate their unions. He suspected that many lovers had also commiserated over a Guinness or two.

"Well, looks like you got it wrong, Conrad." Agatha gathered her purse. "I appreciate the gesture, though. Kent, you're looking smashing." Her voice hung heavy with sadness.

"I'm sorry, Agatha." Kent truly was unhappy that he

had to reiterate the breakup. Now Agatha had to deal with it a second time, once again in front of Conrad.

Conrad stepped up to be the knight in shining armor and walked her to the pub door. Kent watched him close the conversation with a hug before returning to the table. His friend signaled for another two beers.

"No, thanks. I still have mine." Kent pointed to his drink.

"I will need both. You've got a lot of explaining to do." Conrad was beside himself. "I feel like a—"

"Look, I appreciate what you tried to do. It was just with the wrong woman."

"Wrong woman? So there *is* another woman. You sneaky devil."

"Be quiet. I was not two-timing anyone. That's more your style."

"Low blow, but true." Conrad motioned with his hand. "Go on. Tell me who has your attention locked up."

"Doesn't matter. I haven't called her like I said I would. She's not the type to sit waiting in the window. My second-guessing has been my Achilles heel."

"Okay, I'm switching hats from the love doctor for re-kindling romance to love doctor for the scared and pet-rified."

Kent had to laugh at Conrad's silliness. Years ago, they'd made vows to be ladies' men. So far, he was not quite the Casanova. But for the next hour, he spilled his guts about the woman who didn't know that she had control of his heartstrings.

Chapter 9

After an hour, when Kent had wound down his retelling, he felt emotionally drained—and he was missing Dana.

"So you really didn't call her?" Conrad appeared to relish his counseling role. He'd barely interrupted Kent, only whistling when Kent said something that blew his mind.

Kent shook his head.

"You've got to call her before you head back to the U.S."

"I will."

"You're leaving tomorrow morning. Why are you dragging your feet?"

"I shouldn't have mixed business and pleasure."

"It's not like she couldn't have said no. I think, at twenty-eight years old, she knows what she wants."

"Doesn't matter. I should have showed restraint. At least I should have waited until I was done with the project."

Conrad shrugged. "Why didn't you?"

"I thought that if I did wait, well, maybe, she would have

changed her mind." Thinking on his feet came naturally. But having Dana on his mind left him a bit befuddled.

"You can't be an Essex boy, run with the wolves, and now try to act like one of these stuck-up sods. What you're feeling is sheer instinct. Deep in the gut action and reaction." Conrad sat back. "Didn't think that I'd see the day when you lost a lot of your bark. Not a bad look—the kinder, gentler teddy bear."

Kent could do without that nickname from his childhood. His woolly, overgrown afro, pudgy body, combined with a ferocious personality, had made him unforgettable. Once he had turned the corner in his life, he'd been determined to never go back. His mother had spent too many nights wondering where he was and if he'd come back home in the same condition as when he'd left.

Conrad slapped his shoulder. "I'm asking about Agatha. Don't pretend you didn't hear me."

"What about her?" Kent didn't want to talk about Agatha. She needed to remain in the background where he pushed most of his past. Conrad didn't say anything, just wore a sheepish grin. Realization hit him. "Oh, my gosh… you?" His laughter echoed in the small pub.

"Okay, it's not that funny. I have always thought she was attractive. Then, when you broke up, well, you weren't here. She confided in me." His friend paused, still miffed over Kent's amusement. "I listened."

"Oh, brother. Don't try to pretend with me that you're the sensitive soul. 'The Red Fox' was your moniker."

Although his friend's hair had darkened, the youthful version of Conrad had had fiery red hair that spoke to his Irish-Scottish background. Freckles covered most of his face, especially his nose, which somehow attracted droves of women. But it was his wicked grin that slew lots and should've warned them that he was up to no good.

"I didn't push her to talk about you and her. I didn't

want to play magistrate. No, we talked about her—dreams, wishes, her plans." Conrad held up his hands, all signs of hilarity or irritation gone. He stared at Kent, eye-to-eye. "Nothing happened between us because I always thought you'd get back with her, regardless of my feelings."

"And you were willing to let us get back together, even orchestrate it?" A part of him felt as if he should be concerned that his friend had feelings for his ex-girlfriend. Should, but didn't.

"I expected that you would get back together. I mean, why not? She's got beauty, style, and independence." Conrad cupped his half glass of beer. "I may have had to give you some distance, though."

"Does Agatha know how you feel?"

"Heavens, no. Unlike me, she didn't have optimistic harkening that this was going to be a joyful rekindling. She's talking about moving north. I want to make my move to change her mind."

"Look, Agatha and I started on the same line of this race. Then she wanted to switch to the fast lane, something that I wasn't ever planning on. So I do wish her well. And I appreciate you being honest." Kent held up his glass. "I'm not going down that road, ever again. I'm an all-or-nothing person. If I can't give it my all, then that answers the dilemma."

"Cheers, my friend." Conrad clicked his glass to Kent's.

"Cheers."

"On an honest note…Kent, you need to get your house in order. Don't let fear rule. It's not your style."

Kent left Conrad, who he could tell wanted to get on with the new turn of events in his favor. He halfway wished that he'd be around to see them hook up. However, he'd procrastinated long enough with his own life.

Time to head to the United States. Hopefully, he wasn't too late to set things in motion.

* * *

Three weeks had felt like two years. Kent had to admit that he was glad to be back in the U.S. Instead of stepping into the hustle of New York City, he'd headed to upstate New York. The gold-embossed invitation from Grace was equal to a subpoena for a court appearance. Actually, he preferred that setting for the reception that would allow him to see Dana. The confines of her grandmother's private party should prevent any outward signs of her anger. He quite expected to be assaulted by her hurt over his absence.

Although there was no gated community in the area, as he'd heard about for the well-off and rich, there was a definite difference when he crossed the invisible line to where large estate homes lined the city streets. These houses from the 1930s, which were built for the creators of iconic companies and their loyal executives, became a part of the city's historic landscape. While he had left a rainy London, here, the sun was still high and bright, as if it was fooling him into thinking he would receive a cheery welcome.

The Meadows estate, not even close to the property from his Essex Estate days, didn't disappoint. The home had the air of Hampton Court, King Henry VIII's favorite home. Maybe Grace's regal style had also transferred itself to her architectural choices. Though it wasn't overly large by mansion standards, the home was noteworthy for its elegant grandeur and expansive grounds. He looked forward to seeing the interior—and one woman in particular inside.

His taxi was stopped by a uniformed attendant who wanted to see his invitation. After an intense scrutiny, the invitation passed muster. One look at the limos and sedans with their uniformed drivers and he almost wished that he hadn't turned down Grace's offer to send him a car to pick him up at the airport. Cocktail dresses and fine suits walked ahead of him. At least he had selected his best and finest custom-fitted suit so he would blend with the business elite. With the exception of his well-traveled suitcase, he could hold his own among them.

Turning down Grace's mode of transportation was one thing. Turning down her invitation for him to stay at the house was not accepted. To assuage his objections, she promised that he'd be kept busy, as she wanted to finalize details for Dana's ascendance to the throne.

"Welcome, Mr. Fraser."

"Hello." Kent didn't expect to be recognized.

"I'm Leona, Grace's assistant."

"Ah, good to meet you." He shook her hand. Meanwhile, a man stepped up to take his suitcase.

"Would you like to see your room and then join us? Richard will show you the way."

"Thank you." Kent followed his guide up the grand staircase. Guests were milling around on the first floor in small groups. It looked like he would be the new one in the bunch. This is what he wanted and what Grace had promised—she would introduce him to her circle so he could grow his business. Hopefully, she wouldn't think their arrangement one-sided, since he was still working through his own motivations with Dana.

Kent continued to follow his silent guide down the hallway toward the back of the house. Richard opened a door and stepped back for him to enter. Then he stepped through and placed the suitcase on a luggage stand. The room was not overly big, but was furnished with dark, heavy pieces polished to brilliance.

"The closet is here, if you'd like to hang your clothes."

Kent nodded.

"Bathroom is here."

He nodded again and waited for Richard to leave the room before heaving a sigh. A plus of staying in a hotel was being able to unwind behind a closed door. In Grace's house, he felt confined to social etiquette and good behavior.

Sounds of the party from outside his window drew his attention. He walked to the large windows and pulled back the curtain. His room overlooked a terrace, from which a few guests took advantage of the beautiful weather and the long daylight hours to chat and admire the manicured grounds. The faint sound of a piano being played also floated up to him. Hiding out in his room wasn't an option, he knew, so he freshened up and then headed down.

He scanned the large foyer for the familiar face that had held hostage his every thought. A waiter offered him a glass of champagne, which he declined, preferring to keep a level head when he finally met either Meadows woman.

As if he'd conjured her, the guests parted a clean path for Grace to walk slowly toward him. He noted a cane in her right hand, supporting her efforts. He hurried over to lessen her exertion.

"Kent, finally in the flesh." She offered her free hand and clasped his.

"Grace, it is good to see you."

"I wouldn't think that was the case, given your disappearing act," she rebuked him, while smiling as if she was welcoming another guest simultaneously with the winning hospitality of a concerned hostess. "Walk with me."

Kent offered his arm. She patted it, but didn't use the support.

"How are things going with Meadows Media?"

"Very well. My analysis is complete. The good news is that there is high level of confidence in the organization from the lower rungs of the company through to the senior management. Even a light exploration among her peers and competitors are favorable."

"Good to hear. Now, what's the flip side?"

Kent looked at the guests enjoying Grace's hospitality and probably their good fortune at earning an invitation by being on Grace's good side. "You want to cover that now?" he asked.

Grace followed his gaze. "You're right. Tonight is for Dana." She patted his arm. "And for you. Let's go meet a few of my colleagues."

As Kent met each person, he mentally stored information about that individual and his company. It was amazing how quickly the coolness evaporated when Grace not only introduced him, but endorsed his business. No amount of phone calls and testimonials would have cracked the door for him in the same way. He never understood why Grace placed so much trust in him. Everything she had promised had happened so far, with a bit of his help, and he hoped that he could fulfill his part.

Grace finally left him to his own devices. By then, Kent's face hurt from smiling so much and, if he wasn't mistaken, two women had flirted with him. Hopefully Grace hadn't minded that he had used her as a barrier to the women's overly friendly behavior. He did think Grace was going to box one woman's ears when she had loudly chided, "Don't keep your boy toy all to yourself."

"I see you've met Delores Hightower." An elderly gentleman in a suit that looked more off the rack than designer, stepped up and put his arm around Kent's shoulders. "I'm Henry, Grace's husband. You must be Kent."

"Yes." Kent hoped that he'd hidden his shock. He'd pictured Grace's husband as a mirror image of her, sort of a "Biff and Buffy" type, elite, snobbish, and acting terribly affected. Instead, Henry was like an outsider in his clothes, demeanor, and attitude. For Kent, he was a breath of fresh air.

Henry led him away. "You look like you're stepping into the quicksand of all this brown-nosing." He bumped him with his elbow. "Trust me, I've been doing this for years. I've got an escape plan. Works all the time."

Trusting Grace's husband was a big step, but the twinkle in the man's eye promised a bit of comic relief and mischief. After having been on his best behavior for the last hour, Kent relished a bit of fun. He gladly accompanied the older man to their mysterious destination.

"We'll head to the terrace through the study. Do you smoke?"

Kent shook his head.

"I don't, either. Except I've got a fine cigar and I just want one smoke. We'll have to hide behind the hedges or Grace may hit me with that cane."

Kent laughed, immediately liking the patriarch of this family. The room designated as the study was cozy, filled with books, and had an enormous fireplace. Clearly, the place was Henry's man-cave.

Henry opened double doors that led outside. As Kent stepped out, he noticed that the area was privately cordoned off by trimmed hedges. Sounds of laughter and lively conversation drifted through to their hiding place, but there was no sign of guests. For the first time that evening, Kent relaxed.

"Take off that jacket and toss it over the chair. All the airs and graces, no pun intended, are not allowed in here."

Kent didn't need a second prompt. He shrugged out of his jacket, tossed it aside, and then loosened his tie.

"Help yourself to some brandy."

"I'm okay." He was relaxed, but still wanted to keep his head. "But I'll pour you some to go with your cigar."

"Now, you're talking."

They sat on the patio enjoying the evening and listening to the orchestra playing outside.

Finally, Kent spoke up. "I'm waiting for you to ask me about Meadows Media and Dana."

"That company is Grace's baby. I'm here to support and lend an objective ear. But I don't meddle. I trust her instincts and my granddaughter's abilities."

"How was it to live in the…?" Kent didn't know how to say it delicately.

"In Grace's shadow?" Henry turned to him and pondered the lit cigar between his fingers. "I loved that woman from the first time I met her. She lit up my life and continues to make life interesting. I had my career as a math teacher for over thirty years to keep me busy. After a bit of heart trouble, I've had to take it easy."

"Then, you don't need that." Kent took the cigar away from Henry and dropped it in his glass of water.

"That's what I get for talking too much."

"You know, we've got to head back."

"Why?"

"We're missing dinner." Kent's stomach protested, long and loud. Plus, he still hadn't found Dana.

"All right. Time to head out to the brown-nosers," Henry said.

"I can't see Grace putting up with brown-nosers."

"Depends. My lady is a crafty soul. Don't underestimate her intelligence and that gut instinct that she relies upon." Pride crept into his description of his wife.

They reentered the main area of the house, which was largely empty, then followed the sounds of the party into a large, formal dining room.

"Well, Kent, we must take a moment to chat again. I enjoyed that."

"I'm here for a couple days."

"Grace told me. You know where to find me." They shook hands and went their separate ways.

Kent looked around the room for the familiar face. Damn it. Where was Dana? How could she miss her grandmother's reception? His invitation didn't sound as if *he* had had the option.

"Mr. Fraser."

"Yes?" He looked down at the maid standing near him.

"Grace has requested that you sit next to her." The maid led the way to the table, as though no other response but "yes" was in order.

Kent followed her and passed faces that were curiously taking notice of him. He passed several vacant spots to the empty chair next to Grace's.

"Have a seat. Figured that I need to keep you out of Henry's clutches. Before you know it, he'll have you smoking those stinking cigars."

Kent couldn't hide his surprise.

"Didn't think I knew?" She laughed. "The man continues to forget that there are security cameras everywhere." She waved at her husband who cheerfully waved back, blowing her a kiss. His height, girth and shockingly white hair made him stand out in this crowd, but Kent suspected that he'd do that in any room.

Kent debated on popping Henry's bubble or letting him cluelessly enjoy his sinful treats.

"Ah…finally, Dana is here."

Kent's attention snapped to the doors. Call him biased. Her entrance was powerful and her strides were purposeful. All eyes were on her, following her progress into the room.

"Sorry I'm late."

"Have a seat." Her grandmother wasn't pleased.

Dana complied. The entire time, she hadn't looked in his direction. He wanted to wave his arms and say, "I'm here!"

Now that Dana had arrived, Grace addressed the group. Kent noticed that, in her speech, she didn't confirm that Dana was the CEO-to-be, only reiterated her acting CEO title. From Dana's expression, she noted it, too. A few times, her gaze did shift, seemingly unwillingly, over him. It didn't linger, but slid past as if he was part of the room décor. There was not much he could do, with Grace talking to him about his business or the man on his other side inquiring about his contacts.

After dinner, guests said their goodbyes. Kent remained in the main area, standing next to Grace and Henry, as if he was an additional host. Finally, Dana made her way past them.

"Tomorrow Kent and I will be going over his full report," Grace said.

"Yes."

"I'd like you to be present. We have much to discuss."
Dana nodded.

"Let's have a breakfast meeting. Kent is staying here."

"What?" Dana looked at him, not with interest, but with horror.

"I've invited him to stay. Like I said, we have much work to be done." Grace smiled up at Henry. "Besides, Henry has taken a liking to Kent."

"Yes, I have." Henry came over and thumped Kent on his back.

"That's pretty cozy." There was accusation in Dana's declaration. "Guess I will see all of you tomorrow." She kissed her grandfather's cheek and then Grace's before leaving.

"I'll walk you to your car." Kent didn't want to waste any more time with the deep freeze treatment.

"No need. I live on the grounds."

"Oh."

She headed out. Grace and Henry said their good-nights and headed upstairs. Grace looked weary and her loving husband assisted her slowly up the stairs.

Kent took that moment to slip out the door after Dana. He knew the weekend would be spent with Grace, but he had to speak to Dana and make things right. She'd already hit the path that must lead to her house. He hadn't noticed any other building. Although the main house sat close to the street, the grounds behind extended for several acres.

His feet noisily crunched on the gravel. She had to know that he was following. Yet she didn't turn.

Not that he was complaining too hard. Each angry stride worked her hips and turned the narrow, black skirt that brushed above her knee into a sexy, revealing costume. The gravel didn't impede her heels as she strutted down the path and around the corner. Following the same progress, he came upon the cottage, probably originally a guesthouse.

"Dana, wait, please." Calling her name didn't slow her down. If he wasn't mistaken, her pace picked up. "It's good to see you."

"Really?" She stopped and whirled around to face him. The outdoor lighting revealed the anger blazing from her eyes and her body, rigid with contempt. "Well, you've seen me. Now go."

Kent searched for the right words. "I'm sorry for not contacting you, cutting myself off from you…" He took a tentative step forward. "I knew that I'd crossed the line. And…" Another step forward. "I didn't want you to think that I make a habit of…"

"Having one-night stands with your clients?" Her hands fisted on her hips. "Why wouldn't I think that? You did exactly that. Now, you're kissing up to my grandparents. And I have to play along to become CEO. Well, maybe some things aren't worth it."

"Don't say that." He reached out to her.

"Don't touch me." She backed toward the front door. "I'm jumping through hoops. And you're testing out the merchandise."

"Do you think so little of me?"

"Did you give me a choice?" Her voice softened with all the hurt that he'd leveled upon her.

"I screwed up." He chose to be honest. "I screwed up and getting space helped me to think about us."

"All by yourself. Didn't you think that I may have had doubts? I put my guard down, too. Well, I hope you have your ticket."

Kent frowned. "Ticket?"

"The one for you to go to hell." The door closed in his face.

Chapter 10

Dana didn't want to send Kent anywhere. She wanted him right there. But her pride had taken a ding and she couldn't let him off the hook so easily. Fighting the impulse to hear him out and readily accept his excuses, she stood her ground, working hard to push him away. One minute more and she'd have folded against the soft brown eyes full of regret. One minute more and she would have hugged him in a fierce embrace. But he'd heeded her final order and left. She rested her forehead against the closed door.

"How was the party?"

Dana turned to face her mother, who was curled up on the couch sipping hot chocolate.

"I decided not to crash it."

"We all thank you." Dana knew that her mother wasn't the only one of the Meadows family who could stir trouble. They all thrived on drama at gatherings. Showing off in front of the business community would have been a big mistake. The family didn't act in a way that would harm the company—an unwritten rule.

"Doesn't look like it went well."

"Why do you say that?" Dana helped herself to hot chocolate and curled into the opposite side of the couch. Many people remarked that she resembled her mother. She'd accept that if they were talking about physical attributes. Similarities only went so far. Her mother was Grace's youngest, "the unexpected one," as her aunts would constantly taunt. Maybe Grace's age when she gave birth to Elaine, combined with her company's meteoric rise and successes, had given Elaine a lot of time alone, without her mother's heavy-handedness. Her sisters blamed Grace's babying of Elaine for her eventual bohemian lifestyle.

"You walked in looking stressed and ready for a fight."

Dana shrugged away her concern. "Just work stuff."

Her mother sat up and set down her cup. She scooted until she was close enough to put her arm around Dana's shoulders. "You look a little worn around the edges. No one is more suited for the massive job you've undertaken. I am proud of you. But I don't want this job and its mounting responsibilities to eat you alive."

"I'm fine." Dana knew her mom's true feelings were that anything heavy in life wasn't worth doing. She believed that one should have some cosmic connection with one's job, like the bond between soul mates. Her constant quest for such an experience effectively had removed her from her family during Dana's teens. It took gurus in India, tribal priests in Africa, and motivational speakers in the Caribbean to put her on her personal path. Three years later, she'd returned home to open a coffee shop and run an open mic for local singers and spoken word talent. She and her long-term boyfriend figured this was their calling until their souls said otherwise. At no time did their communication with their inner selves seem to tell them that Elaine had to raise her daughter.

"Sweetheart, your heart is important. Love feeds the heart, not stress and constantly meeting someone else's expectations." She ruffled Dana's hair. "You used to want to be a ballerina."

"I was...like, six." Dana hated the dreamy speeches her mother frequently delivered. There was a time to be practical and grown up. Somehow, her mother and boyfriend fed off each other and ignored that same belief.

"You were so graceful. I know there are pictures somewhere," her mother continued, as if Dana hadn't spoken. "Wonder what would have happened if your grandmother didn't take you under her wing."

"You left me, Mom." Dana didn't want to have this conversation. They'd never broached how she'd felt when her parents left her—first her father and then her mother. Her grandmother also refused to discuss it out of concern for Dana's feelings. "She had no choice but to take me under her wing."

"Well, she did a fantastic job, don't you think? For the most part. If I had my way, I'd much rather you be in the coffee shop than running that massive company. Let one of your other cousins deal with it. They lack imagination, so let them toil at the job."

"Mom!" Dana slipped off the couch. "Where's Ronald, by the way?" She hoped they both weren't crashing at her home.

"He's trying to line up judges for the talent contest. He sends his love."

"Where did he go to find these judges?" Dana was not used to seeing her mother separate from her constant companion.

"He's in Florida, but he's coming in tomorrow and then I'll be out of your place."

Dana nodded. Good news on both fronts. "I'll head up to bed."

"Good night, sweetheart. Remember what I said. When in doubt, choose love."

On that disagreeable note, Dana headed up to her room. If she lived her mother's philosophy on life, she'd be broke and unhappy. She didn't have to live the mega-rich lifestyle, but having a little money in her pocket did relieve some worries. Her mother relied too heavily on emotions, although she did manage to return home with remarkable timing for a cash infusion.

"Choose love, indeed." Dana muttered all the way to her room.

After preparing herself for bed, she slipped under the covers. Her cell phone rang. Who would be calling at this hour? She grabbed the phone and read the display. Her grandmother?

"Yes, Grandma."

"It's me. Kent."

She knew it was him from the minute he said that first word.

"I'm using the house phone."

"It's late." She pressed the phone to her ear.

"Don't hang up. Hear me out."

She didn't respond. Instead, she hugged her pillow and waited for him to continue.

"A month ago, my life seemed pretty ordinary, going according to plan. Even when I had the contract for Meadows Media, I expected to come in and do my job as usual. Maybe a few unexpected things would pop in on the business side, but nothing that I couldn't handle."

Dana snuggled closer to the pillow. His voice—warm caramel syrup.

"Except that I didn't expect to meet you."

"You knew I was the head of the company."

"Yes, but I didn't expect to be drawn to you beyond a working relationship. You're a beautiful woman, but having the chance to see you working and thinking, evolving as a leader, well, I found that sexy as the dickens. I wanted to know more about you, the person under the no-nonsense business demeanor. The more that I learned, the more my respect grew for what you are undertaking and how you are handling it all."

"All of that sounds good if what you think you know is the truth."

"You doubt that you're a leader?"

"I'm not Grace. Grace knows that I'm not her. I'm afraid that I'm here until she can devise a better role for me. I know she wants me involved, which is some comfort."

"If it helps, I believe in you."

Dana closed her eyes. The message was softly spoken, touching all the right spots. Why couldn't he have said this before disappearing to London?

"See you in the morning."

"Yeah." She hung up and stared at the wall. All her defenses had crumbled into tiny pieces. With every point that Kent made, a brand-new landscape emerged. Did she have the courage to take the next step?

She understood the turmoil of emotions and rules. Maybe if he hadn't been the one to go into self-exile, she might have done it. She sighed. At least he'd returned and sought her out to explain.

Dana drifted to sleep with a contented smile.

"I'm glad that you made it on time." Grace signaled to the maid to serve the coffee.

"Good morning, Grandma." Dana didn't mind the mild jab at her tardiness last night.

"Good morning, Grace...Dana." It was Kent. Dana nodded at him. His wink brought a warm blush to her cheeks.

"Let's get started." Grace was all business.

"I have the analysis of the report." Kent distributed copies. "I'll give you a few minutes to review the information."

Dana pushed aside her plate. She'd been enduring sleepless nights wondering what her employees thought of her. After reading it, she found that page after page of information confirmed some of her suspicions. That felt good. On the other hand, critical comments were frank, some a bit personal, and all were piercing in their indictments.

"Share your thoughts, Kent."

"The good news is that the company's employees have transferred their loyalty to Dana. They see the transition as seamless and have confidence in Dana's leadership."

"Senior management isn't necessarily unanimous." Grace read through each page, sometimes going back to a previous page to reread.

"I'm sure that I can guess who had a say with some vitriol." Dana was ready to pummel O'Brien.

"It's all anonymous."

"Sure it is." Dana didn't figure that Kent would share the dirty details on who said what, anyway. "I'm not sure that the current team is one that I will stick with."

"What do you mean?" Grace lowered the report. Her demeanor turned frosty.

Kent intervened. "Well, before we get to that, there are some other details in the report worth noting."

Dana was done tiptoeing around an obvious solution. "I mean that I want to pick my own team."

"Those people have been loyal for years."

"Loyal to you."

"There's no need to jump ahead. I'm sure that reorganization isn't automatically necessary." Kent distributed more analyses.

"I do not want anyone kicked out of the company." Grace rapped her knuckles on the table.

"I need people that I can trust."

"You need to elicit that trust."

"Why? Because that's the way you'd do things?"

Grace glared at her granddaughter, who wasn't backing down. "Yes."

Dana turned to Kent. "Have you written up your recommendations for how I can improve my team's efficiency? I'm sure there is something in there about having the best employees in place to move the company forward."

Kent looked uncomfortable. "Ladies, employees are one component. I think we need to pull back and refocus on the complete picture."

Grace took a deep breath and motioned with her hand for him to continue.

It took a bit longer for Dana to get her emotions in check. Pressure had mounted until she popped and spouted a verbal and emotional flood of words that she was sure she'd pay for later. Grace didn't care for meltdowns.

"I'm sorry." Grace reached over and squeezed Dana's hand. "Continue, Kent."

Dana had to bite her cheek to keep from smiling. His look of surprise was too priceless.

They managed to get through the remainder of the report without too much dissension. Clearly, the different divisions under Meadows Media had various needs and the market conditions weren't especially kind right now. Dana knew that would be the next hurdle as she examined what would soon be hers.

"Well, Kent, I must say that you've done an excellent job with identifying Dana's attributes, the company's perception of her and a broad overview of Meadows Media. What do we need to focus on in the immediate future?" Grace turned her gaze toward Dana. It was apparent Grace expected him to address her shortcomings.

"One thing that is noticeably uneven is the media's and competitors' image of Dana. Yes, she has to fight against the idea of nepotism, but she must also come across a bit more—"

"Aggressive," Grace provided, with a stern nod.

"Assertive," Kent countered.

Dana didn't mind either word. She'd already come to terms with the fact that she might have to wield her strength with organizational management to get her way, which Grace did with sheer guts and panache.

"I suggest that she goes to media training."

"Wait a second. First, I have to go to your leadership summit and now this? I don't have time." Dana wanted to bang her head against the table. *When would the grooming end?*

"This is more than a nine-to-five job, Dana."

"I'm not worried about rolling up my sleeves and working long hours. But there's got to be some breathing time."

"You know the saying that you can sleep when you die. Think of that as your breathing time."

Dana's mother's words came back to her. But she dared not contemplate anything that Elaine said with regard to the business.

"The key is not for you to transform into Grace. Your strength comes with a quiet power. You can make someone completely at ease. You quickly win them over with your intelligence and confidence in knowing your information." Kent pointed out all the attributes on his fingers.

"So then, what's wrong?" Grace looked at her as though she was a test case that had gone haywire.

"When challenged, she gets defensive," Kent remarked in a flat voice.

"I do not," Dana declared.

"She reacts impulsively."

Dana balled her fists and forced herself not to respond to his criticisms.

"I see what you mean." Grace nodded her understanding. "How do we tame her?"

"Grandma—"

Grace raised her hand. "No need to contradict everything that Kent is saying or anything I suggest. Kent, I'll put her in your hands to work on that." She pushed back her chair. "Come. There is something else we must all discuss. Maybe it will help matters."

Dana looked at Kent for a hint. His curious frown showed that he didn't have a clue what Grace meant. The three walked in a staggered line to Grace's office. Dana knew the room well, since Grace's lectures about Dana's various transgressions were held in there. When Dana needed a retreat, she headed to her grandfather's study, which was like an oasis to relax and bounce back. Dealing with her grandmother's disapproval was tough and its effects long-lasting. Like when she had snuck out with friends to get a tattoo on her ankle. That almost brought on more than a lecture, but she was saved by the fact that the tattoo depicted praying hands with the word *Grace* under them. Her cousins wondered why she'd waste a tat on their grandmother's name.

Dana took a seat in front of her grandmother. Despite all that they'd gone through and the many times that they'd butted heads, she loved Grace very much. Although earning her displeasure didn't have a limit, on the rare occasions that Dana won her approval, she could float on the power of her grandmother's smile.

"Have a seat, Kent." Grace indicated the chair next to Dana's. Her mouth was tight.

Dana sat up in her chair, nerves on edge. Her grandmother was clearly perturbed.

"All this talk about perception is on point." Grace pulled out a file and placed it in the center of the desk. She swiveled it around and opened it so that they could look at it.

There, in crisp color, were photos of their kiss in New York City, permanently rendered. Dana closely meshed in Kent's arms. Her eyes closed. Her arms wound around his neck. And all the other feelings that the camera couldn't capture. The warm longing that had coursed through her body. His rigid contours pressed against her. His arousal, sprung strong and provocative against her pelvis. His mouth had been a sweet harbor of scintillating devices, including an expert tongue and exacting lips. An intimate moment now turned common and reckless.

"Oh, my." Dana's face was heated to a scalding temperature.

Kent made a sound that might have been distress or indignation.

"I don't quite know what to say. Mild flirtation, this is not." Grace looked down at the contents and then up at them.

Kent began, "The only thing that I have to say is that I would have wished that I'd been able to tell you about this before you received these photos."

"I see nothing to apologize for." Dana folded her arms. A wave of defiance rippled through her.

Grace pursed her lips. She remained quiet, looking at each of them as if trying to delve into their minds. "I do not want this blowing up in the press. I paid a lot to get these when one of my news contacts gave me a heads-up that an eager freelance photographer was looking for a buyer."

Dana didn't care about the opinions of the press, especially when it came to her romantic life. She couldn't, and wouldn't commit, to anything. Having her mother around reminded her not to extend her heart recklessly.

"Mrs. Meadows, the only thing that I'm most concerned about is your feelings on the matter." Kent had managed to remove any casual feeling from the conversation. As he had predicted, Dana was more inclined to go in defense mode in such a situation.

As Grace shifted her scrutiny from one to the other, giving each equal consideration, Dana knew that, at any moment, her grandmother would blow. Yet her expression didn't go beyond irritation, but Dana didn't want to trust that there wouldn't be more fallout from the photo.

Grace closed the file. "Like I said, I don't want to see this in the news. You're adults and I have no misgivings on the matter. I suspect that's what you wanted to hear, Mr. Fraser."

"Thank you."

Dana didn't know if now was the time to adjust her grandmother's belief that this was not an ongoing relationship, which it might turn out to be. By now, she had moved beyond her anger over the situation with Kent. But, Dana admitted to herself, there was no guarantee that anything more would happen.

"I hope you haven't bitten off more than you can chew, Kent. My company is a vital part of my being. My granddaughter is a part of my heart. It goes without saying, although I'm telling you, that I don't expect to have to pick up any pieces after you're through with either one."

"Grandma, it takes two. I don't want to put all the burden on Kent."

"Not to worry. I was once young and I remember the beginning rush of romance."

Dana was always tickled to see her grandmother revert to a warmer, softer image. It didn't happen often, but she liked having Grace act human.

"This afternoon, I want to talk about the employees." Her grandmother held up her hand. "I know we have different viewpoints. Let's talk."

After this latest revelation, Dana didn't have a problem chatting over their differences. Grace's accepting reaction still puzzled her.

A knock on the door interrupted them. Grace bade entry.

"Grace, it's Jen," said Leona.

"Is my sister in the house?"

"She is outside inspecting the garden, but will be in shortly."

"Let Henry deal with her. I'll be out soon." After her assistant left, Grace addressed them. "Dana, I wouldn't be putting this much energy into your transition if I didn't think you were the perfect fit. With your additional training and the leadership summit conference coming up, we should be able to wrap up everything before the annual meeting."

Dana nodded. Again, that knot of worry and pressure formed in the middle of her chest. Maybe if she went with the flow, kept her ideas to herself until after she got the job, she'd be less stressed.

She watched Grace exit the room. Who was she kidding? Creating new ideas was how she did her job. Such innovations had pushed Meadows Media, a private company that played against the big dogs and won, into the forefront of the corporate world.

"So, we've been outed," Kent said.

"I don't think it counts when the occurrence is in the past. That was a temporary detour. You're sorry for how you left things. Apology accepted. I'm fine with moving on in our separate lanes. We can get back on track and finish up our business together." She jutted her chin toward the file. Dana turned away from the photos. Those reminders were painful twists to her heart.

"A detour—yes. Temporary—hope not." He gently took her hand and clasped it between his.

"I'll let Grace know that it's over."

"Do you want it to be over?" Kent traced her forehead, trailing his finger down the middle line of her face, past her nose, and down her lips.

Many nights, she'd asked herself that question and answered it as she waited to hear from him. She'd pulled flower petals to decide whether or not to be with Kent. On two out of three wildflowers, the verdict came in: she should choose Kent.

She'd even made the situation a hypothetical case to Sasha, looking for her impartial input. As a hopeless romantic, her assistant had unknowingly rooted for Kent.

"What do you say?"

"Do you work over all your clients like this?"

"Only the ones named Dana Leigh Meadows." He brushed a fleeting kiss against her forehead. "Born on February 7." His cheek settled against her head. "Successor to Meadows Media."

Choose love. "You know I don't do anything halfway."

"That's what I'm hoping."

Dana grabbed Kent's face and hungrily reached for his mouth. Her imagination of a rekindled kiss couldn't have been any better than the real thing. He wrenched away from her mouth and delivered wet adulation to her chin and behind her ear, before she launched her counterattack on his lips.

"Let's sneak away," Dana coaxed.

"Where to?"

"Follow me." She led him out the doors leading to the patio. As he helped her over various garden structures, they giggled like drunken college kids—minus the alcohol.

Chapter 11

Dana felt like a schoolgirl bringing home her first boy-friend to meet her mother. Oddly enough, it was the first time that her mother had met a significant other in her life.

"Oh, hello, dear."

"Hi, Mom." Dana couldn't stop her mad giggling. She kept her hand clasped in Kent's.

"I'm Elaine, Dana's mom. You are...?"

"Kent Fraser. I'm an executive coach, currently work-ing for Meadows Media."

"Well, Kent Fraser, good to meet you. Honestly, I haven't seen my daughter smile like this in a while." She shook his hand. "I've been telling her about mixing plea-sure with a touch of business. Didn't realize that it already was happening. Good for you, sweetheart."

"Mom!"

Kent had a good laugh at Dana's expense.

Her mother primped herself in front of the large mirror mounted in the hallway. "Ronald is coming soon. So I won't be back to cramp your style." She winked boldly at Kent.

A car horn sounded.

"Let's do dinner soon. Love you, honey." Dana's mother hugged her, then she pushed her daughter away and swept Kent up into a tight embrace.

"Good to meet you, handsome. Love the accent. You should keep it."

Dana walked with her mother to the door.

"He's *the* one, isn't he?"

Dana shrugged. Not once had she ever confided the intimate details of her life to her mother. She hadn't ever had so much of a girl-talk moment with her mom. Plus, she didn't want to jinx anything.

"March to your own beat, love." Her mom patted her cheek and headed toward the car, where Ronald waited patiently for the colorful character who was her mother. After Elaine said something to him, he emerged and took big long strides toward Dana with arms outstretched. In one giant scoop, he engulfed her in a bear hug and spun her around as if she was a child.

"Proud of you, kid."

When he was finished, he returned to the car with a satisfied smile on his face at their successful stopover. Dana had stopped reading anything into these drive-by visits. There were no rules about parenting. She had learned to accept what she had, different though it might be. Every time she met her mother and Ronald, she repeated that to herself, hoping one day she'd believe it.

"Are you okay?" Kent came up behind her, molding his body to hers.

Dana shut the door. His closeness, touching his body, having something strong to lean back on, felt good.

"You seem sad."

She turned to face him. "Not really." She shook off anything that might resemble close to dreary thoughts that were a downer. "Can we get back to us?"

"As long as there aren't more Meadows family members about to jump out at me."

"Can't promise that. We are a mighty bunch. Actually, it's my job to bring us all together for Grace's birthday party in November. Now *that* is a bigger feat than leading Meadows Media."

"I'd say that you're up for either job." He hoisted her up with his hands, supporting her butt while her legs wrapped around him. "I'd say that the skills are the same." He peeked around her as he carried her down the hall and up the stairs.

Dana didn't bother to tell him where to go. There wasn't much to the house. Eventually he'd find her room in the tiny cottage.

"On the right." Okay, so she couldn't wait any longer.

She fell away from him onto the bed as if she was about to make angels in the snow. Unbuttoning her top, she wished that she'd worn a blouse that only needed to be slipped over her head. Instead, she ripped open the shirt, sending the last few buttons flying across the room.

Her bra took less time, but still landed in the growing pile on the floor. For every piece of clothing she stripped off, Kent added one of his own. His latest attempt led to him hopping on one foot as he pulled off his sock.

Dana sat with her knees drawn up. Being the first one naked had its advantages. Watching Kent extricate himself from his socks and other clothing was a lovely sight. His muscles at work, flexing and tightening, were like an art exhibit. She preferred his lean physique rather than thick muscles that other men got from long hours at the gym.

Her admiration also took in his tight backside and taut thigh muscles. It was all she could do not to grab his butt every time he walked past her. She was no expert on the intricacies of the anatomy. But she was darn sure that she knew a top specimen, arousal and all.

"Why are you smiling like that?"

"Scared?"

"Depends on what you're going to do?" He playfully shielded his arousal. "You look like you're going to devour me."

She beckoned to him with her finger. "I'm ready for lunch."

"Be careful what you ask for." His voice dropped low and became velvety-soft.

As he eased onto the bed, straddling her, his body felt poised, ready for liftoff. He continued mounting her until she reclined under him.

Dana boldly rotated her position under his body for their mutual enjoyment. The man was desirable from head to toe. She could never tire of his sexual aura. She wanted to savor every inch of his body.

Before she could begin to pleasure him, his tongue set the pace. Hot and wet, he bathed her clit, titillating the nub until she moaned. While his tongue took point, his fingers flanked her opening to tease her labia into submission. She writhed like a woman glad to be under his power.

Flickers of his tongue softly beat a rhythm between her legs. Whatever carnal call he wanted, she was willing to shout. His tongue circled her entrance, warming it up for later. All her blood rushed to fulfill the call, flooding her nerve endings and sensitive flesh.

Softly she touched him, rubbing his sac and planting her mark of ownership on it with wet kisses. Instantly, his body reacted, tightening under her constant onslaught. While he conquered the apex between her thighs, she promised nothing less as she mercilessly teased his shaft. Kiss after kiss, long languishing licks, and suctioning his tip, she aimed to please.

"I'm going to have a blackout if I'm not in you in the next second."

"Well, come on, baby. You're not getting out of this that easily."

She waited impatiently for Kent to slide on the condom before pulling him down onto her. He hoisted her legs practically to her ears and drove his shaft deep within her. Her moans increased with intermittent calls for a harder pace. He pounded. And she sucked him in. Her walls tightened like a mold along his length. She clenched his butt cheeks, digging in her nails, egging him on.

Deep. Hard. To the point.

She didn't know who was sweating more. But their friction had reached combustible levels. Their bodies slid across each other. Her breasts crushed against his chest. The heat they generated triggered a current as strong as a riptide between her legs. No time to think. No time to react.

Her hands gripped the headboard slats. Truly, she felt as if she was floating off the bed. Her equilibrium had malfunctioned. Her body short-circuited. Even her moans had turned into loud cries as she endured repeated spasms of release, in waves of pleasure that were short, long, and anything in between. Her neck arched and she had to close her eyes to keep them from crossing. The man wouldn't stop to allow her to catch her breath. His tongue played with her nipple as she spilled to the last drop.

Only then did he release. She was too weak to endure his torture again. She'd been drained to within an inch of her life. Standing wasn't an option. Sitting would require her to be strapped upright to a chair. All she wanted was to bask in the afterglow of phenomenal lovemaking.

Kent whispered in her ear, "Don't forget our meeting with Grace this afternoon."

"Hush. Get some rest. I may need one for the road."

"Your wish is my command."

Grace didn't hide from much in life. That was not a natural trait, she realized, when she bothered to recollect her younger days. Yet now she stood outside the formal living room where Henry and her sister, Jen, were chatting. Grace suspected that her sister was quite aware that she hovered. Jen never failed to share her critical remarks about her sister to whomever, even to Grace's husband. What could she expect from her older sister who held a grudge for over sixty years, from back when Henry had been her own fiancé?

"Oh, Grace, did you need something?" The maid hovered, eager to be of assistance.

Grace waved away the solicitation, irritated that she'd been involuntarily announced. Pasting on a fake smile, she stepped into the room with a ready greeting for Jen.

Henry was used to his wife's theatrics and ignored her.

"Grace, I was surprised to hear that you had a reception on behalf of Dana. I wasn't informed," Jen remarked.

"Why should you be?"

"The rest of the family does own a sizeable amount of stock. Must I keep reminding you?"

"How could I forget what I gave to the family? What has that got to do with you being informed about the reception?" Grace swept her irritable gaze to Henry. Why didn't he warn her? Jen always had something to complain about. Lately, she was hell-bent on staying abreast of every move in the company. "I wanted my colleagues to meet Dana."

"You can't babysit her forever, you know."

Grace tried to be patient. Her sister was eighty-four and her mind was fortified with steel. They could fight with the energy of teens. But she didn't want to fight, especially not about the company or Dana. Her youngest granddaughter was off-limits when it came to family battles.

Jen didn't heed the no-fly zone. "If Dana isn't the right one, then pick someone better suited. Your eldest daughter, for instance."

"Verona?" Grace turned her steely cold gaze on Jen. "What is the point of this conversation? Has Verona said something that should be shared with me?" It killed her to have to ask Jen if her own daughter had come to her. Crossing into each other's territory had been a constant in their lives.

When it came to Verona, Grace's sister had gone rogue and corrupted her daughter's mind against her mother. At age eighteen, Verona had run off to sing with an R&B group—and Jen had helped her. When she returned home, Verona was pregnant, and gave the baby up for adoption. Even though she orchestrated Verona's eventual marriage to the "respectable" Jasper—with whom she had had Fiona—Grace knew, deep in her heart, that Verona had exacted payback in the most hurtful way.

"She hasn't said anything. I was just looking out for her concerns."

"No need," Grace responded, emphasizing both words with restraint.

Henry cleared his throat. "Jen had a few ideas for your birthday party." His smile wavered under his wife's pointed irritation over his efforts.

Grace wasn't so easily mollified. Tension between the three had overrun the room with swirling hot and fierce emotions.

"I think we should have a movie of the family shown at the party," Jen suggested.

"That's an excellent idea," Henry cheered. He always wanted for her to make up and move on with Jen.

Each time, Grace tried, but Jen's bitterness and her stubbornness were oil and vinegar to her.

"In order to have a family movie, you have to have a family who would cooperate with it." Grace pulled at her sleeves and sniffed. She couldn't guarantee that the family would attend the party, much less go on record to share memories. Every last one of her children had some wound that she supposedly caused or contributed to.

Party or not, she found insincerity or forced exaltations on her behalf repulsive.

"Let me work on it. Please."

"Many hands...Grace." Henry wiggled his eyebrows at her, his not-so-discreet sign for her to play nice. Her dear husband was such a pushover. All of his daughters and even the grandchildren had him wrapped around their fingers. Everyone doted on him too much.

She loved his ability to transcend the family wrangling and issue his mantra: everyone must remember they were family. Maybe that reminder was having negative effects on her daughters, who treated each other with mild interest like strangers on the same train.

Grace reminded them, "Dana is spearheading the efforts to get everyone on board. She's been in touch with her younger cousins. Figured the young people might have the better sense. Maybe you can work with her."

"That's an even better idea." Henry had taken to wiggling his eyebrows at Jen.

Grace coughed to hide her smile at Jen's discomfort. Her husband wasn't any better when he realized what he'd done. Was he looking at her for help? Or was he checking to see if she'd caught him? He was too sweet for his own good.

"Was there anything else, Jen? Is everything okay at the house?" Jen had moved into their parents' home. Well, she never moved out of it. Once they died, she'd taken over the home in a nearby city. Grace didn't visit much. When she had to, the trip was usually brief.

"I have contractors coming to the house to update a few rooms. Nothing too drastic."

Grace listened, with half an ear, as Jen detailed the work.

Many times she wished that their relationship wasn't so strained. All this time certainly hadn't made water pass under the bridge. For decades, progress had been frozen solid, like ice. Grace would admit that it was understandable, given her actions.

Eloping with Henry sixty years ago had sent shock waves into their universe. The cataclysmic event ripped apart lives, dreams and family.

Jen had been the beauty, the one with promise to be married well and spread their genes. She was the one prepped to be a good doctor's wife with hundreds of recipes in her arsenal and a figure that was gorgeous and primed for babies.

While nature gifted Jen with all the fine attributes that a young woman of that time needed, the well was all dried up for Grace. Her hair hadn't grown down to her shoulders. Her features were blunt and wide. Being tall wasn't too bad, but thinness had never blessed her. Whether she ate a lot or not enough, her limbs remained solid and heavy. Her feet couldn't seem to stop growing. "Plain Grace" was one of her kinder nicknames.

Her parents didn't put any stock in her abilities to nab a decent soul. Secretarial school was the plan after high school. After all, what man without major issues would want her? Not even eligible bachelors at church raised a hand to take her to the occasional social function. Her caustic tongue got her in trouble. She couldn't rely on someone to come and sweep her off her large feet. So, the next best thing was to be able to earn a living. Although her parents undervalued her worth, Grace thought this would be the best medicine for what ailed her.

She went to secretarial school, got her skills and a job. Once the money flowed into her hands, she set about gaining her independence. No one noticed or cared about her growing success. At the time, Jen had nabbed a promising pre-med student named Henry Meadows. Their courtship had been vigorously encouraged on a time frame that could give a person whiplash.

Grace had entered college to study business and paid her own way. She spent her time staying out of the fray with her head buried in books. It just so happened that Henry was also looking to escape the whirlwind events that were about to forever change his life.

Several times, they'd bump into each other on the back porch, away from the drama, and head into their soon-to-be private world. He'd commiserate and she'd listen until she felt confident enough to share her opinion.

"Grace?" Henry nudged her back to the conversation.

"I also want to have the garden overhauled."

"Not a problem." Grace was curious as to why the major changes, but she didn't want to show any major interest. Getting into Jen's business tended to end with accusations tossed at Grace about her intervening and meddling. The routine was that Jen would say what she wanted and Grace would write the check—no questions asked—out of her prolonged sense of guilt.

"I want your party to be held at my house."

"What?" This was definite cause for Grace to meddle.

Henry interjected, "Jen is planning to invite a lot of guests."

"Then I want a private party for just the family. Like a breakfast party."

"What?" Grace rapped her cane on the floor. Words were failing her. She needed her thoughts to settle down and her nerves to do the same. Her mouth worked itself into a straight indomitable line. "I can't do that."

"Why not? All you have to do is come and play the queen." Jen crossed her legs. All this time, nature had still been kind to her, with her good health and her seeming agelessness. Her only bitter regret was that she'd never had children. Although several suitors came over the years, she had found fault with each.

Grace couldn't be diplomatic any longer. "I don't want a party in that house."

"It's my house now," Jen countered with a softer approach. "Here is your house, Grace. But *my* house—that's where it all began for us. I feel that it's a perfect place for the family to reconnect."

"I think she has a point, sweetheart."

Neither one of them could understand why Grace didn't want to go back there to celebrate anything to do with her life. Her mother had ripped her to shreds when Grace announced that she and Henry were in love. All her mother's talk about love, Prince Charming, and soul mates had only been for Jen. What she'd saved for Grace had put her in the same trade as women on the street who lived by lesser means. Her mother had never struck her as a child. But that day, the strike on her cheek had left a wound beyond physical swelling and discoloration. Her father had prayed for her salvation and then handed her a suitcase.

Her crime had been falling in love and leaving her sister to be the fodder for small-town gossip.

Grace had worked hard to redeem herself in her own eyes. Job after job, climbing the ranks, earning higher places on the social ladder. When she'd become a mother, she'd hoped that now she was part of a family sisterhood and her mother would open her doors to her. Not once did her mother invite Grace home. When she did visit the house, her mother used Jen to send her away. Her father did meet and play with the grandchildren, but he wouldn't cross her mother on matters on the home front.

Grace never claimed to be a saint. She held on to each hurt, around which scar tissue grew like a thick shield, protecting her from the feelings of rejection. Jen had her own levels of anger, and maybe hate, and went along with their parents' wishes until their passing. Their father died early of a heart attack, while their mother eventually had to be cared for in a home for patients with dementia. Only then could Grace visit her ailing mother without risk of being thrown out of the house. During those visits to the home, she became just a family friend who resembled someone that her mother couldn't remember.

"Grace, dear, why don't you think about it?"

Grace suddenly felt tired. Not sleepy. Not exhausted. Just drained. This unexpected visit had taken her down too many paths to sadness and pain.

"I must get back to work."

Her sister gathered her pocketbook. "I'm not going to back down, Grace. You're taking care of Meadows Media. Well, I'm taking care of the family."

"Dana knows my wishes."

"And she'll be busy trying to step into your shoes. How can she possibly do your bidding when it comes to family matters? As complicated as they are." Jen scooted herself to the edge of her chair. "And I expect that you want everyone to show up."

"Okay, ladies, no need to fight over the *family*. We're all under one umbrella."

Grace always knew that Jen would turn the screw one notch tighter.

Chapter 12

Dana sat in front of her mirror, witnessing a transformation from a regular person who happened to be working at the top of Meadows Media. Within the hour, she had undergone a metamorphosis. Additional hairpieces added volume to her styled, gelled tresses. Her makeup was layered on thick to even her skin tone, accentuate her best features and mask any unflattering parts.

At Grace's insistence, an entire wardrobe was custom designed just for her. She didn't believe in buying off the rack or accepting clothes from designers. Everything should denote quality and exclusivity. Dana didn't quite buy into that philosophy, but she also didn't mind having clothes that perfectly fit her body.

"We're ready for Miss Meadows."

Dana followed the program director to the main stage. She listened to the instructions and hoped that she'd be able to recall them when the time came. Her heart thudded against her chest. When she looked down at her blouse, she could actually see the pounding against the fabric.

"Let's get you into position."

Dana joined the panel that also was settling into place. This morning show covered news, local business, and light celebrity gossip. She introduced herself to the other panelists, who included a local chef who made it to the final round on a televised competition, the CEO of a local bank, and the owner of a hair products store.

Kent and Grace had decided that it was time for Dana to step up and conduct interviews. For the better part of the months in which Dana had been acting CEO, Grace had still conducted any interviews. Not having to be interviewed certainly took the pressure off Dana, but left her vulnerable to criticism that she wasn't ready for the scrutiny. Kent had prepped her for media attention and how to answer any tricky questions a host might throw her way. A few local interviews would allow her to test her abilities, check her response when thinking on her feet, and gauge reactions from people who didn't have a vested interest in impressing her. The program director signaled for them to get ready. The countdown began. In less than five seconds, the news would start and then switch to the host for the business segment after a short commercial break.

Dana kept a smile on her face, even when the camera wasn't on her. She'd seen enough blooper reels to know that you never relaxed until you were safely in another room. Plus, she wanted to give off the impression that she was calm and a pro at this type of interview. The board meeting was in less than a month. When Grace made the announcement, Dana wanted to be seen as the next generation to successfully take on her grandmother's legacy.

Another commercial break started. Their segment was next up. She listened to the host make the introductory remarks. Her gaze pinned each guest with eye-to-eye contact and a curt nod. Before she came on the program, she'd thought they would bring in all CEOs of similar types of businesses. Dana's stomach immediately started to churn. How to predict what questions would be asked? "LaSalle, let's start with you. You're a local cook."

"Yes. I started at fast food and then worked my way through many kitchens. I tried out for the show and got in. Yeah!"

The hostess asked, "Has anyone here been to his restaurant?"

They shook their heads.

"I'm sure when you win that final you'll have a line going out the door."

"What about you, Mr. Caphorn? You have opened branches of your bank all over our city."

"And that's a good thing. Accessibility and number of branches or ATMs make a difference."

"With the slam that banks have taken, why would anyone start one in this economy?"

"It's exactly in this economy that small banks that cater to the community are warranted. We can be flexible to meet the current market needs and switch things around faster than any corporate bank with crazy fees."

"Miss Meadows—"

"I'm interested to know why we can't get an audience with Miss Meadows," Caphorn interrupted. "Why not use a community bank for all your financial needs? I'm sure we can help each other."

Dana looked at the hostess, then back at Caphorn.

"I was going to ask who designed your fabulous attire, but now I'm interested in Caphorn's suggestion. So, what of it? Can I be the matchmaker for your two businesses?"

This blindsiding question knocked her back a bit. While

some might have found Caphorn's brash approach appealing, the style grated on Dana's nerves. If he truly wanted her business, instead of making a spectacle of himself, he could have talked to her after the show.

"I do believe in helping businesses grow. I support the Chamber of Commerce and all that it does to help business people like us to network with one another."

"But Meadows Media. Seems like they close ranks."

"What about you, since you were brought in over many others, to this show? How do you feel?" The hostess addressed the owner of the hair products store.

"I had to build my store from scratch." The woman tossed Dana a nasty look.

"I earned my way to the top," the bank manager said.

"Well, Miss Meadows? What do you have to say to those who think that the path to success should be as easy as yours?"

"I'd say that you shouldn't judge unless the soapbox you're standing on can withstand the same scrutiny." Dana turned to the owner of the hair products store. "Each company had to start somewhere. Meadows Media was started by one woman, my grandmother. She cared for it the way you care for your store. She put in long hours to make it successful, like I'm sure you're doing. When she found something that worked, she followed through with it. When it didn't, she let it go." Dana leaned in on her elbows. "But unless you're planning to live forever, I'd say that you'd better have a succession plan in place. My grandmother did. It happens to be me. Qualified and able to do the job." She turned her undivided attention to Caphorn, who had recognized too late that he had entered dangerous waters. "Our leadership hasn't changed hands often. Hasn't been bought out by anyone. Hasn't changed its last name since inception. While I'm at the helm, the staff will remain loyal and hardworking."

"And on that note, we'll head to commercial. When we return, we talk to Dana about taking on the large responsibility of being acting CEO."

Dana could barely wait for the director to signal a commercial break, then she addressed the hostess. "I was under the impression that this was a news interview. For the community. Not a reality show face-off."

"Not to worry. You're all doing fine. Love the dynamics," the hostess remarked.

No one else spoke during the break.

"And we're back with spotlight on business owners and the feisty successor to Meadows Media. Must be in the DNA, won't you agree?" Everyone laughed, except Dana.

She couldn't toss off the silly comments, the leading questions, and their naïve thinking that she couldn't handle herself. She could do more than handle, she could shut it down.

"Ah, Dana, we actually have confirmed reports from employees who wish to remain anonymous that they have grave reservations about your leadership," the hostess said.

Dana pretended to fix her clothes and looked at her watch. They had bled over into the celebrity news. She guessed she just found out who they were going to target. Irritation continued to build.

"Anything, Dana?"

"You want me to address faceless reports? Meadows Media isn't a fortress where, once you've come in, you can't get out. Employees are valued. Loyalty is rewarded. If the two conflict, then my advice would be to seek employment elsewhere."

"So you're putting your staff on notice."

"No. I'm addressing again the nameless and faceless

reports that you toss at me." Dana sat back in her chair, folded her arms, and determined from that point that she would no longer respond to any questions.

The cameraman couldn't get enough of her scowl. No matter how hard she tried not to look in the camera, at the monitors, she was clearly giving him a piece of her mind with each glower.

By the time the interview was over, Dana pulled off the mic, gathered her things and left with her mini entourage. As she was leaving, Caphorn tried to make nice—much too late. The chef tried to shove a box of samples in her hand. Dana flicked her wrist over to Sasha who took the treats, but wisely kept them out of Dana's reach. The trash can was only a few feet away.

Dana exited the building. Someone called her name.

"Miss Meadows, I want you to know that I think you will be a marvelous business leader. You'll make us all proud."

Dana remembered the TV intern who saw to her beverage requests when she'd arrived. Dana offered a nod. She handed the college student her business card. "If you should need anything…"

"Your car is over here." Sasha touched her elbow to guide her in the right direction.

"I don't want to be interviewed by that woman ever again. Didn't we ask her what the topic would be? This didn't feel like a general overview. Not in the least." Dana was still seething.

"We will send a letter to the television network." The newest addition to Meadows's PR staff piped up.

"Why don't you have a follow-up feature on the Meadows Business Network?" Sasha suggested.

"I don't want to come across as desperate. I'm not running for public office." *Public perception*. She hated those words.

"It's Grace." Her phone had been ringing. She knew that her grandmother would call, especially since Dana had so casually tossed out that those who didn't like her could quit.

Dana took the phone. "Yes, Grace."

Her grandmother sighed through the speaker. "It could have been worse. Let's wait to see what the fallout is." Then she hung up.

Her grandmother hadn't taken her to task. She hadn't issued any condemnation over the matter. Only then did Dana relax as she entered the car.

"Is everything okay, Dana?" Sasha said from where she sat beside her. She already knew that Kent's criticism wouldn't be so accommodating. He wouldn't want to wait to see what the fallout would be. His philosophy was that you should never set yourself up to be a target. His philosophy would say that she wasn't ready to be CEO.

Sasha said, "Emails are coming in, requesting you on several shows. I wouldn't recommend many of them, but there are a few good, meaty ones. I'm sure by the end of the day, you'll have a ton to pick from."

By the time Dana reached her office, she was revved up and in high spirits. Her dark mood had lifted. She was ready to dive into work for the remainder of the afternoon, which included lunch with the mayor, meeting with the human resources and legal departments, signing her approval on personnel realignment—with Grace's blessing—and then an industry-sponsored dinner.

Still no word from Kent about her TV show appearance.

By eleven o'clock, she was steamrolled. She was beyond exhausted and couldn't wait to take a quick shower and hit the bed. She and Kent had played phone tag all day. His dance card also seemed to be filling up with the results of Grace's endorsement at the reception. As a result, time spent in each other's arms had been far too infrequent for her liking.

She walked into her house and kicked off her shoes. The scent of hot chocolate wafted through the air. She sniffed and followed the trail to the source. Kent was at the stove stirring a pot with a red apron tied around his waist without another stitch of clothing.

"What are you making?" Dana's mouth watered because it smelled so good.

"Real hot chocolate."

"Looks rich and will keep me up at night." She saw the remaining chocolate bars on the counter.

"Trust me. I'll have you sleeping like a baby."

Dana rubbed his naked behind. The only thing shielding his front was the red apron. "What if I'd brought home friends?" She giggled at the thought.

He shrugged. "I took the risk." He poured her a glass of wine and handed it to her.

She kept a hand on his behind, pleased to see a rising bump in the front.

"Your bath awaits you."

"Really? But you didn't know when I was coming home."

"I have my methods." Kent kissed her lightly and scooted back when she tried to reach behind the apron.

"Sasha! I must talk to her," Dana remembered suddenly.

"Then you won't get surprises like this." He returned his attention to the pot on the stove and moved it onto a cold burner.

Forget Sasha.

Dana continued sipping the wine. She discovered the

small plate of crackers and sliced cheeses. What had she done to deserve this?

"For your first interview."

She looked down at the neatly wrapped box now lying on his palm. Many thoughts and emotions ran through her mind. One especially had hold of her, a fantasy of what-ifs. She didn't dare think about that now or put words to what she could barely allow herself to imagine.

Tentatively, she pulled apart the wrapping and then opened the box. A beautiful string of pearls lay against velvet matting.

"My mother always said that a string of pearls added a touch of class to any picture or look. Ever since I met you, I am continually amazed by your tenacity and brilliant mind."

"You're making me blush."

"I'm not offering false compliments. You're one classy woman and I wanted to give you something that, when you wore it, would remind you of us."

He looked ready to continue, but restrained himself.

"I'll go jump into the bathtub." Dana couldn't stand there another minute without bawling. She didn't doubt for one second the sincere note in his voice when he'd spoken. But he didn't really know her, just the parts that needed to be shown to run Meadows Media. No one stuck around her for long. They came in, attracted by the glamour of her social status, latched on like a barnacle to a ship and then moved on, but only after she kicked them out of her life. None of that description fit Kent. But there had never been enough substance in her personal life that would keep him for the long term. She fingered the pearls, a symbol of class, the new identity that she wanted as CEO.

"I left room in the tub so you could fill with hot water to warm it up, if necessary."

"You know, you're too special." Dana was overwhelmed by his thoughtfulness.

"Only when it counts."

The air between them went from casually romantic to erotically charged in an instant. What was he offering? To ask would mean the answer was important to her. More than important—kind of life and death for her soul. Dana hurried to her room. Her exhaustion must be causing this wave of sentimentality to settle. It felt good. She could learn to like having a man around, someone to come home to at the end of the day. Having it all—a career, family, and a man—was an idea that she didn't usually entertain.

Men came and went, never fulfilling her needs, never complementing or balancing her. She'd learned not to expect anyone to ever step into the role. In a way, she'd convinced herself that she didn't need anyone permanent to fill the void.

Family was out for that position. The Meadows clan could only be taken in small doses. In the past, it had been easier to avoid the usual drama with a distraction like her internship at Meadows Media, which she had had before coming on as a regular employee.

She sat on the edge of her bed, staring at her closed bedroom door. On the other side was a man whose job it was to fix her. In the process, his coaching strengthened what she knew to be deep inside herself. Maybe that's why she'd fallen so hard for him. Her fingers curled into the sheet. The realization hit her with the impact of a pillow to the head, not hurtful, but with enough momentum to seize her breath and send her in a dizzying spin as she fell back onto the bed.

Love. She loved Kent Fraser.

"How's the water?" he asked at the closed door.

She sat up in case he came in. Everything had to appear normal. She had to act as though he had not reached the inner sanctum of her heart. To hand over her feelings was to surrender her independence, her ability to think straight. The women in, and close to, the Meadows family—Grace and Henry in particular—were stark examples of their handling and mishandling of love.

"I'm now going in." She stripped out of her clothes and reached for the thick plush robe that she was sure hadn't been in her closet before.

Off-white lit scented candles greeted her as she walked into the small bathroom. Candles decorated the surrounding surface, emitting the delicate scent of vanilla. Flickering flames provided a warm glow in the space. She didn't know how many candles had been used for that effect. But it worked to add to a magical, ethereal scene that allowed her entry into its world.

The invitation to sink into the warm water couldn't be denied. She filled the remaining space in the tub with hot water, poured in a liberal dose of cleanser, and grabbed her spa pillow. Now for the music. And she'd be all set.

"I've got your hot chocolate." Kent knocked at the door.

"Why are you spoiling me?"

"Consider it a reward."

"For a job well done?" Dana slipped off her robe and stepped into the water. Her body sighed as much as she actually did as she sank under the suds. The R&B songs playing in the background helped her relax as the singer crooned about the one who got away. She adjusted the spa pillow and leaned back.

"Aren't you coming in?" she asked Kent.

"No. I'm here to serve you." He offered a small teacup of rich chocolate.

"This is so decadent."

"I got the recipe when I was in Milan. They think our

hot chocolate is revolting because it's diluted with water or milk."

She sipped the mixture that looked thick enough to dunk strawberries in. Her taste buds exploded with the warm elixir. Its smooth texture and rich chocolate flavor made her want more.

Kent kissed her, swiping the excess chocolate with his tongue. This small, helpful act wakened her longing. Not that it ever slept around Kent. Her body was always on heightened alert in his proximity.

"You need to make this for me again." Dana wiped the cup with her finger, feeding herself and then Kent. He sucked her finger clean and added a kiss on her mouth as a final touch.

"Time to wash up." He took the sponge from her and squeezed the shower gel on it. "Your arm?"

She raised her arm for his attention. Each stroke across her skin sloughed away the exhaustion of the day. His arm slid against her as he continued to attend to her body. She leaned forward for her back's turn. Heaven. He spared no inch of her skin.

"I might need your services more often," Dana moaned.

"My pleasure."

The man definitely had the skills of a spa attendant. Her every muscle had been stroked into submission until she was completely relaxed.

"Water is cooling. Do you want me to refresh it?"

"No. I'm wiped out." She bit back a yawn. Before she could gather the strength to push up out of the tub, he scooped her out. The water drained off her body. With little exertion, he walked to the bed and lowered her onto a towel that was laid out. He dried her off, applied lotion, and slipped on her pajamas.

She reached up and pulled him down toward her. "Stay the night?"

He kissed her, long and deep. "You need your rest. You've got another round of interviews. This time, keep your emotions low-key."

"I did fine." She wasn't being cocky, but she had managed to take charge of the interview. "And I didn't need the media training." She curled up against him, her leg thrown carelessly over his. "We can count this one as a practice run."

He cuddled next to her. She nestled in the crook of his arm. A state of drowsiness settled upon her. She hoped that he did decide to stay the night. He'd made it a sweet, romantic way to end her day.

Kent waited until Dana fell asleep. He listened to her breathing, waiting for it to grow deep and even. His pride had burst when he saw her on the TV. Her confidence had certainly grown in a short time.

She wasn't far from the possibility of falling into self-defeating traps, though. The interview questions would get more challenging, more personal, to incite a reaction from her. Working with Dana had tuned him in to what her triggers were. The minute the interviewer asked a question, he knew what Dana's reaction would be. He'd hoped that an internal brake would have activated her restraint. That's what he feared the most. That, in proving herself to him, to her family, and to the world, she would adopt an overly aggressive attitude to demand respect.

She sighed in her sleep.

He liked watching her sleep. Her face was calm. Her problems didn't seem to weigh as heavily on her as when she was awake and her brow was knit with deep creases.

"I will do whatever is in my power to help you get this

job," he told her drowsing form. He'd do so with the limited time that he had, with the board meeting in less than a month and Grace's expected final announcement bestowing the CEO title on Dana.

He didn't know why Grace had not come down on them with red-hot anger after the television interview. And he knew that she wasn't playing spectator on the sidelines.

No, he was being judged by Grace. What the rules were, he didn't know. More importantly, was he capable of doing the right thing, for Dana and for Grace? He could only go by his ability to read people and staying in tune to their needs.

Chapter 13

"The mother of all interviewers wants to talk to you." Leona danced around with the information.

"How many more of these I have to do?" Dana stretched her back. She'd love a massage and wished that Kent was around. He'd gone back to England to prepare for his upcoming leadership summit. The idea of seeing him on his home turf dulled the edges of disappointment at her empty bed for the past few evenings.

"The annual meeting is in two weeks. Hang in there."

"The announcement is *expected* to be made. Grace is going quiet on me. Haven't seen much of her."

"You have got to understand that the upcoming weeks are just as difficult for her, maybe more so. It's like another child that has grown up and she must move on."

"Are you her defender for life? What are you going to do once she's retired? Are you interested in a job here?"

"No. I have been with your grandmother for fifteen

years. The job came to me at a time when I needed something solid. Grace had a knack for taking in the broken and mending them."

Dana looked up to see if Leona referred to her. No, instead she had drifted back to that time when Grace had been an employer, but also a mentor.

Grace, Kent, Dana—they were all broken in some form.

"Does Grace want me to do the interview?" Dana asked.

"She's not voicing her opinions. I think that Henry has stepped in to make sure she goes through with everything, including taking her helicopter hover-mode out of range."

"The old girl must be panicked." The idea didn't bring any humor with it. Her grandmother also had to face her future, the next phase where she had to come to terms with moving aside—and staying there—until her last breath.

"I do think that you should conduct the interview. That's mega-news. Wait until you're back from the summit. It'll be your exclamation that you aren't second best."

"I am." Dana leaned in and whispered, "I cannot replace Grace. She was the best."

"She was the best for the times when she led and within the context of her history. You have more avenues to either create a niche or to enhance the big services. And you can be the best at that. So, don't ever say you're not. Besides, they will eat you alive if you do."

"I used to think that I wanted to be like my mother. Pretty. Happy. Sailing through the world in a bubble of good cheer and certain self-indulgent madness."

"Elaine could have been a part of Meadows Media, if she wanted."

"I wouldn't have thought so. But I've come to realize that my mother did many things and took many of the actions that she did to dispel any notion that she had the intelligence to be a part of the company. She knew that saying no wouldn't save her from enlistment."

Leona said nothing.

"It didn't save me," Dana admitted.

"You were about thirteen when we first met."

"I gave Grace so much hell." Dana had apologized many times to her grandmother for being so spiteful. She'd felt so betrayed by those who were supposed to love her.

"It was nothing more than Grace probably did at your age. I keep telling you that you're alike." Leona chuckled. "You've got the brain, but you've also got grit."

"Grit." Dana had gotten so used to seeing Leona that she couldn't fathom not having her around. Grace's personal assistant had seen it all, heard it all. She had filled the space between her mother's absence and Grace's passion. Everything Leona said came with a certain sadness that, like everyone else, she was also moving on with life, taking that turn to the next phase to travel the world at a leisurely pace.

"That's what it took to build and keep this company for so many years. And it's what it'll take to go full steam into the twenty-first century."

Dana didn't doubt the grit part. But one day, Grace would be gone. Whether she had ruled by fear or from respect, she held the family in its place. Right now the gates were rattling, for they smelled fresh meat. Those who felt overlooked wanted to make a play. Those who didn't care, but didn't have a voice, wanted to be heard. Her cousins hadn't ever called her this much for any girls' night.

"My world is changing." Dana glanced at her email inbox that blinked almost every second with messages. Her phone never stopped ringing. Her office now had a small closet for clothes, as she was usually either headed off to impromptu meetings or hopping a flight to one of the company's subsidiaries.

"That's why you are the future."

"Gosh, that sounds trite."

Leona shrugged. "It's the truth. Listen to your gut."

Dana leaned back in her chair. She stretched out her legs on the desk and crossed them. Her gut was a greedy machine. Her ego wanted Meadows Media. Her heart wanted Kent. The race was on and she hated to think that only one could win. She hated to consider that she'd have to choose.

"I'll do the interview, but with Grace." Dana looked at Leona. "Like you said, let's make this the exclamation point."

"I'll check with her."

Dana didn't move after Leona left. The impact of what she had said still reverberated. What to do with the company in the twenty-first century? Already she had a few ideas. She wished Kent was around to knock around the scenarios.

"Dana, I've brought a package for you." Sasha stood in the doorway, grinning so wide that her eyes looked closed.

Dana stood to take the unexpected delivery. The mail run had already been done for the morning. "Why didn't you open it?"

"It's not mine to open," Sasha said and walked out of the room still wearing that smile.

The package sat on her desk unopened for several minutes. Finally, she pulled it close. There was no return address. Still, she was sure Sasha knew who'd sent it. She'd hoped that a return address would have revealed Kent as the sender. Disappointment stung.

In short order, she broke the seal around the box. The potent, concentrated scent of vanilla hit her nose. Yes, this was a gift that was meant for her to open. She continued opening the box. A dozen candles of various shapes, all vanilla-scented, were in the box.

A small white envelope lay on the top with her name neatly written on it. She set down the box, zeroing in on the note.

A reminder that I am always thinking of you— Kent

The vanilla scent covered the small note. With eyes closed, she held it to her nose. What she wouldn't give for a vanilla-infused bath and a wonderful back rub afterward. Taking her time, she removed each candle from the box and placed them around her office. She wanted them to surround her. No matter which direction she turned, she wanted to see them.

Not one day had gone by when she didn't wear the pearls Kent had given her. Some days, she wore them around her neck. Others, she wound them around her wrist like a fashionable bracelet. Once she'd even worn them in her hair, looped around her ponytail holder. In some ways, she treated the jewelry like an engagement ring.

She looked at her naked finger and closed her hand. Wishful thinking never got her anywhere. Like all the other secrets and private wishes she had stored over the years, she managed to squeeze in one more.

Kent, to have and to hold.

"Till death do us part," she wished. With a sigh, she took the note and slipped it in her drawer.

Time to get back to work.

"Kent, I don't need a washing machine." Despite her reservations, his mother circled the washer-dryer set and opened the washer lid.

There was no mistaking the satisfactory nod as she inspected the depth of the tub, the various knobs, even the little drawer mechanism for the specialized detergent and clothes softener. The dryer earned more than a nod. Her smile emanated as she checked the list of attributes the manufacturer claimed.

"It's yours." He turned to the salesman to give him the information.

"I can't. I really don't need a new one. Your stepfather already bought one."

"Not as good as this."

She looked back at the duo. "You're right that it's not as good. But it's what I need." She turned to the salesman who sensed that he wasn't about to make a sale. "Thank you, young man."

He stalked off with shoulders rigid and no backwardly hopeful glance.

His mother shook her head and turned to him. "Now, it's time I get home."

Kent sulked all the way to her house. He couldn't understand her growing reluctance to accept anything from him. Alister didn't help either, making it difficult for her to take his gifts.

"I still don't understand." He'd parked in front of the house. Rather than go in and stay for dinner, he'd prefer to head home to his empty flat. Right now he was too irritable to hide his hurt and frustration. While he felt that his stepfather deserved to know how much he hated that he'd brainwashed his mother, he didn't want to create a spectacle in front of his step-siblings, who managed to look up to him, unlike their father.

"Why did you marry him? You didn't need to marry him to get out of the estates. I would have gotten us out. I was this close."

"Is that what you think?" She'd opened the door. Now she sat back in the seat and pulled the door closed. The car's interior light revealed her shock. By the time it got dark again, she seemed rigid and eerily calm.

"Mum, you and I were a team. We got past the big bad wolf." He made an attempt to lighten the mood.

"Yes, we did. And still life was hard. But I met Alister and I fell in love when I didn't think I had any chance of ever feeling that need to hope, trust and care again." She cupped his face. Passing cars' headlights caught the tears hovering on her lids. "But I did. I fell in love with a man who had no pretense about him. He was a mechanic and will be that until he can't work." She turned toward the house. "We have many things. And we don't have quite a few. What we do have is love."

Kent didn't want to see his mother cry. He had spent too many years doing that. Even after she had divorced his father, she continued to be sad. He'd never felt so useless. What could he do? He had spent his days thinking how he could get them out of the estate flats and into a family home with him and her, the survivors. That was his job, as man of the house.

He'd set about his new job by working harder than the rest. He studied harder and focused. His goal had never changed. When his mother introduced him to Alister, he barely regarded him as a threat, or even anyone worth re-membering. He was a plain mechanic with a divorce and kids under his belt.

Kent had warned his mother that Alister was only com-ing after her for a live-in babysitter. It was the only time that she'd banished him from her presence. He'd apolo-gized, still confused by her divided loyalty.

"And I don't need money." His mother had learned to outmaneuver his logic. "I truly am doing fine. I know it's not the big castle-style house that you wanted to buy for me. I know that Alister is not Prince Charming on the grand horse. Those were your dreams, son. None of it matters when you're in love."

Kent snorted. "If things weren't neat and tidy, then love wouldn't last." He didn't feel the need to elaborate about how the loss of a job created a trickle-down effect to loss of goods, unhappiness in the house, frustration with the family until the relationship suffered.

"Come in and have a cup of tea."

Kent shook his head.

"Please. It's my anniversary."

Kent wanted to kick himself that he'd forgotten. "Nine years. Congratulations."

"We're hoping to do something for our tenth."

"Sure, Mum, I'll come in and have a toast."

"Good."

Kent had never lived in this home. By the time Alister had started dating his mother, he had already been on his own. No memories with Alister had been created to erase some of his childhood disappointments. It came at a time when he'd headed off to university and wasn't there to vet his stepfather and maybe develop the trust that his mother wholeheartedly had in Alister.

Nine years should be enough time to know if Alister was up to no good. No matter how hard Kent looked for faults, he couldn't find any. His stepfather might be rough around the edges. He might have not gone to university. He might be covered in grease by the time he came home. But he made her happy, took away the tired, drawn look around her eyes.

Alister opened the door as they approached. His mother ran into his arms.

"Kent picked me up from the supermarket."

"Great. Joining us for dinner?"

"Only a quick drink to toast your anniversary."

"Come on in, then. The kids should be here shortly, if you'd care to stick around. I overheard one of them saying they're bringing a cake." He rubbed his hands together.

Kent stuck around longer than for just one toast. Seeing his mother's joy kept him there. Maybe it took falling in love himself to recognize its power. What he'd thought he was doing by outdoing Alister with gifts was no more helpful than if he was the other man intruding on a happy couple.

Observing their life that was unencumbered with a lot of material trappings, Kent found himself wanting a bit of what his mother and stepfather had discovered.

Peace. In the middle of it all. In everything around the house and holding the family together, there was a state of contentment.

"Why do you constantly look so sad?" Camille asked her son.

"It's not sadness, my dear," Alister answered for Kent.

His mother looked up at his stepfather.

"Dare I say it's a woman?" Alister asked.

"What?" His mother's hand covered her mouth.

His step-siblings, who had just arrived, hooted at Kent's discomfort.

"Is that true, Kent?" His mom looked like he was withholding some sort of good news. "You have a girlfriend? Why didn't you tell me?" She pulled him into her arms. "I was so worried about you. Wondering if you were working too many long hours. You're not eating. A bag of bones, if you ask me."

"I'm eating, Mum. More than I need to."

"Well. Tell me about the girlfriend."

His stepfather chuckled. "You need another drink?" He poured a shot of brandy without waiting for an answer from Kent.

"She's not really my girlfriend. It's not her. It's me."

"Go on."

Kent explained all about Dana. As he talked about her, he couldn't hide the pride he held for her. But like he'd said, this gray area around his feelings wasn't about her. He tried to subdue much of his emotion, but his voice betrayed him. The embarrassing flush that heated his face gave him away. A full family discussion on the matter wasn't his intention.

"She sounds absolutely fantastic. I want to meet her," Camille declared after Kent stumbled over the details.

"She's in America," his stepfather reiterated.

"Actually, she'll be here in a week. I'm hosting a leadership summit as part of my executive coaching program."

"Really!" His mother clapped her hands. Her excitement lit up her face. Her expression brightened. "I can't wait." She hopped up and started talking about where things needed to be moved to declutter the room.

"This is what I get for opening my mouth," his stepfather muttered. "Now I'm going to have a list of tasks for your young lady." He grinned and thumped Kent on the arm. "But I can't wait to meet the woman who put a spark in those eyes."

As Kent drove off later that night, he wondered if he'd crossed an important milestone. One where he was ready to acknowledge that Dana had nestled in his heart the way she loved cuddling next to him. All his theories, on love and how it worked or didn't work, had been blown to bits when Dana entered the equation. That's what scared him.

Chapter 14

Dana had never visited London. Like any big-city international airport, Heathrow offered her first view of the ancient, but very modern, metropolis. The port was a mix of cultures, accents, and seemingly nomadic travelers. Once through customs and baggage claim, she encountered a driver holding a placard with her last name.

At first she thought that she'd be sharing the ride with the other attendees, but no one else joined them. Before long, they had melted into the traffic and wound their way through the city and its roundabouts.

Dana felt like a child in a toy shop as she peered out the car window to take in the neighborhoods of row houses, tall apartment complexes, patches of green parks and very old buildings. She couldn't wait to see Buckingham Palace, Big Ben, the House of Commons. But after she had had her fill of all the touristy spots, she wanted to go deep into the very British world and enjoy a pint, chat in a pub, find examples of Shakespeare's literary mark on the city. She had to admit that she had been ecstatic to see that they were staying in a refurbished noble's palace-turned-conference center.

Two hours later, the van finally rolled to a stop. The bellman opened the car door and assisted her from the backseat onto the red carpet that led up the stairs and through the entrance of the conference center. He ran ahead and held the door open for her to enter.

"Welcome to the Brownwyn Resort and Conference Center. Please proceed to the check-in."

Dana thanked the man who was dressed in a suit that was reminiscent of something in the late 1800s or early 1900s. Whatever era the clothing was from, it had added to the quaint surroundings that probably had more history in them than she could remember from her school days.

Considering how much this leadership training seminar cost, she shouldn't have been surprised by her room. Suites were her customary accommodations when she traveled. She still had a hard time adjusting to the sense of importance that others placed on her because of her job title. But this room was beyond a suite. This apartment, where she'd be living for four days, was as big as her cottage.

Her schedule didn't have her meeting with the group until that evening for a welcome reception and then dinner. She wasn't overly tired and didn't plan to take any naps to help deal with jet lag. She could stay in this massive room and feel a bit alone or she could go exploring the grounds.

A knock on her door stopped her from getting a drink to quench her deep thirst.

"Yes?" She looked through the peephole, then emitted a surprised whoop and threw open the door to jump full-force into Kent's arms.

"I came to see if you survived the long flight."

She couldn't quite put her finger on what was different about him. Whatever it was, he looked gorgeous.

"It's so good to see you." She couldn't stop kissing him until he was heartily laughing.

"How am I going to keep my hands off you this week?" He clasped his hands behind her back, holding her prisoner between his arms.

"Close the door because we're not going anywhere. My body has been going into shock, not having you in me." Dana jumped up and wrapped her legs around Kent.

"I don't think I can make it to the bedroom—wherever that is in this massive place."

She whispered into his neck, "I don't want you to."

He laid her gently on the sofa with its olive-green paisley print. He could have laid her on yesterday's newspapers and it would have been fine.

She removed her clothing, stopping in the middle to undo his pants, before going back to her original task.

They were both in a frenzied hurry, bumping heads, giggling while singly focused on one another. Their efforts landed them on the floor. Dana knew that the man whom she loved was here, with her, right now. Nothing else mattered.

Kent liked to think of himself as chivalrous, but today, he couldn't be bothered with waiting for Dana's permission. While she'd shimmied his pants down to free him, he kissed her hard. Her fingers grabbed hold of his shaft.

"I can't believe that I'm this lucky...." His voice hitched, exertion mixing with passion. "It can't be luck that I've met you." She worked his shaft, playing with the tip, coaxing its surrender which she completely controlled.

Dana took a deep breath. "No, it's not luck. I feel too connected to you."

He shifted back to admire her, an act of which he never

tired. He covered her breast with his hand, moving his palm back and forth against her nipple. She squirmed every time there was contact. He kissed her soft, tender flesh as his response, branding her mound with its dollop of brown with a searing sweep of his tongue.

She brushed his tip against her inner thigh and he almost howled. His legs were weak as desire drained energy from his muscles. He reached for protection, which she took from him and used to cover his length.

Once more he kissed her, playing with her mouth in a heated dance. As he led and took her in, she led and played with the tip of his tongue. While his tongue explored and conquered hers, he lowered his hips against hers, sliding into her.

She twisted and squeezed her hips against him. Each move allowed him deeper access.

Harder. Rougher.

Pounding from soft to hard, from slow to quick to frenzied.

Even his pulse joined in on their bodies' chaotic, happy dance. Whatever the theme of their symphony of the flesh, he only cared that he was with the partner who mattered. Legs intertwined. Arms locked around each other. Their bodies writhing against each other.

"I want it harder," she moaned. Her teeth ravaged his shoulder.

He gritted his, loving the sharp pain mixed with knee-buckling pleasure. She was positively wild and feisty. Whatever she needed, he satisfied, with enough gusto to cause her to gasp for breath.

Holding on with one hand on the back of the sofa and the other on the armrest, he used those as his anchors to work his lower half deeper. Her fingers found all the deep grooves between his muscles and teased him mercilessly.

They rocked together, generating a heat index hot enough to scald them both. As she writhed back and forth, his hands held down her hips to cut back on the movement, which had him crossing his eyes.

In one swoop, Kent picked her up and stood. He moved forward until her back was against the wall. There, he finished what he'd started. Long strokes in and up. Their guttural moans in each other's ears, wild and feral. He didn't stop repeating the motions—in and up—until she sealed his mouth with a kiss as she came, shuddering against his shaft and inviting him to join in the release.

With a fierce growl, he followed her lead. *Was it safe to admit that he was in love?*

Kent opened the leadership summit with twelve CEOs and a few CFOs. The event was a biannual assembly of representatives of top companies from a wide range of industries. On the surface, their needs didn't match, but many aspects of running any company were similar. In this intimate setting, he hoped to bring together bright minds, known mavericks in their respective fields, to stimulate new ideas.

Dana was the only woman at this, the third anniversary of this event. It wasn't like Kent didn't have enough pressure as it was to have a successful meeting, but he had to do so without letting on that he and Dana were a couple. If she didn't stop making dreamy-eyed expressions and boldly winking at him, he'd be caught hankering after her.

For four days, the attendees worked through case studies. The intensity of the classes matched coursework from graduate-level business administration classes. None of the assignments could be done as a solo project.

Kent caught Dana's frustration at having to work with people whom she hadn't necessarily chosen. Or, in some exercises, she did choose people, but their performances were less than stellar for the assignment. He hoped that she got the underlying lesson, which was about learning to handle the various dynamics that make a great team.

As a surprise, the guests were invited to sit in on a management meeting of a billionaire airline tycoon. Kent wanted to show that, in the real world, even in bigger companies, they would encounter some similar issues faced by smaller corporations. The key would be to pick the battles, choose what was important and remember the vision, the mission, the objective.

Dana quickly picked up on the lessons to be learned. She turned off her whining, volunteered for the most challenging projects, and did a lot of listening. Kent found that he couldn't be more proud of her efforts.

"Where are we going?" Dana looked out the car window and then at Kent. "Are you kidnapping me?"

"I wish that I could. I'd find my own deserted island and hold you hostage."

"As long as we have double and triple doses of lovemaking every day, I'll stick with you."

Kent didn't want to tell Dana where they were going in case she freaked out. Telling her that they were on their way to meet his mother and stepfather might cause a touch of distress. Now that he thought about it, not telling her could also result in a blow-out.

"I want you to meet a university friend."

"Oh, cool."

"And my family."

"Oh, wasn't expecting that. Suddenly, my stomach is churning." Dana blew out a noisy breath and wrapped her arms around her waist.

"They are really cool. You'll like them, I promise."

"Any siblings that I may run into?"

"Laci and Ben are my step-siblings, but they couldn't make it, though they send their regards."

Kent paused midspeech, paying keen attention to Dana's mood. He truly didn't want her to feel pressured. Although his mother had prepared a full-course meal with steamed pudding and custard, he would come up with an excuse if Dana couldn't handle the attention. But he'd jumped ahead with his plans because, in comparison to meeting several members of the Meadows family, having Dana meet his family should be no big deal.

When they arrived at Alister's house, he parked the car, slowly walking around to her side and opening the door for her.

"Will you hold my hand?" she asked. He readily took her hand, which felt as if she had been holding ice cubes. He raised it to his lips and kissed each fingertip.

The door opened and his mother ran out to greet them. She looked dressed for church. He could only imagine what poor Alister had to wear.

"How can you have a dinner without me?" Conrad stepped out of the house, as well. Though he wasn't dressed in a suit, his clothing was definitely not his usual athletic gear.

Kent felt proud of his family and best friend, who clearly wanted to put the best foot forward for Dana. Their efforts meant a lot to him. It also put him at ease as he made the introductions when they finally entered the house.

His mother beamed at him. When she could not help herself, she hugged him and whispered, "I think this might get Alister on a plane to America."

Kent looked over to his stepfather, who was comfortable with Conrad, but still a bit shy with Dana. It didn't matter. For the first time, he felt like he had the makings of his own family.

Chapter 15

Almost as soon as Dana arrived home, Grace had scheduled a follow-up interview on a local TV show. Dana had done enough interviews by now that she could read how the hostess received her, the company and even Grace. Something hadn't sat right with her, from the time they had done the pre-interview chat about the questions the hostess would ask, especially those about her appointment as president and CEO of Meadows Media, which Grace had recently made official, up to when the cameras started rolling.

Though Dana had never met this woman, there was venom in her eyes. Whenever they made eye contact, she transmitted bitterness and anger. Since Dana was the only one being interviewed, there was no one around she could ask.

From the first question the hostess had asked to the present one, the inquiries were loaded, ugly and manipulative. She didn't care about the normal answers. The hostess had dredged up Dana's past jobs and relationships, as if trying to commit a character assassination in the process. And now she had moved on to Dana's company.

"Meadows Media is losing its founder. Grace has been a beacon for the company, but also in this city, not to mention her impact in business and as a philanthropic icon. Her legacy is beyond measurement. Tough footsteps to follow in, wouldn't you say? I mean…where have you earned your stripes without Grace's help? Not that I'm critical, mind you. But, what do you hope to bring to Meadows Media, as the next generation?"

"Wow. You've tossed a lot of questions at me. Looks like you've already answered them, too. So I'll move onto the more substantive inquiries. I have the same entrepreneurial spirit that my grandmother has, but within today's context of digital technology. I plan to make the magazine digital-only eventually. But more immediately, I plan to create an online young adult magazine."

"Really? I guess with your young age, you are more likely to recognize that segment of the market."

"Let me clear up that faulty logic. With my business experience, I can identify what population segments are underserved in the media and who needs a break-out publication just for them."

"Anything else that your qualifications have availed you of?" The interviewer dropped her overtly fake, saccharine smile. Instead, a brittle edge coated her words.

"There will be restructuring and consolidating within the company."

"Buzzwords that mean job elimination."

"I see that you have a tendency to try to outthink me. I have no intention of destroying jobs. There are partnership opportunities where the best of both worlds can be shared and exploited among companies."

"Sounds like Meadows Media may need to buckle up for a bumpy ride."

"I like an employee base that isn't settled with the status quo."

"I guess time will tell whether Grace Meadows made a sensible choice. She did build her company from scratch and put her life's blood into making it a success, not only for herself, but for the city, as a tax base, source of stable employment, and significant contributor to local charities."

"You're a bundle of hope and well-wishes," Dana said sarcastically. "You keep checking on me and waiting for the sky to fall. I don't live my life in that manner. So, unless you have something substantive to ask, this interview is done."

"What on earth was that?" Kent asked when they were back at the office.

"She plucked my nerves," Dana responded.

"Why?"

"What are you asking me?"

"Why did you let her get to you? She is not the person you have to convince. The public is watching how you handle yourself and her. You came across as an arrogant knucklehead."

"Knucklehead?"

Kent couldn't stop pacing. For days, he'd felt as if Dana was trying so hard to exhibit her readiness for the CEO title that her efforts were backfiring. He'd also noticed that she was pushing him away. Excuses about work. Excuses about not feeling well. First, he blew it off, thinking that she was sick, but it hadn't gotten better.

Watching the business news was how he'd learned about the interview. He knew the personality of the various hosts, but Dana wasn't listening and his suggestions were met with a brush-off.

The talk about business strategy made him get up to go get a beer. Something told him that she hadn't cleared anything she said in this interview with Grace. A news program wasn't the place to unveil business strategy.

Dana operated like a solo act.

"What is your problem with what I'm doing? I'm not mincing my words. I have a vision. And I'm going to make the company even more successful and relevant."

"Why are you unlearning everything?" Kent asked exasperatedly.

"I'm not your performing monkey, Kent," Dana snapped. "I was never yours to control and bend."

"I'm a coach, not a puppet master."

Dana shrugged. Her body language was clear, indicating that she thought the two were synonymous.

"Have you talked to Grace?"

"About what?"

"I'm sure you blindsided her."

"Oh, now you're an expert on what Grace thinks?"

Kent stopped his pacing. He couldn't continue if he wanted to. His mind had gone blank. His motor skills hung in suspended animation. A roar sounded in his head, leaving him wounded and hurt.

"We're having a fight," Kent said.

She snapped her finger and pointed at him as if it was a gun. "Brain cells do work."

"Why are we having a fight?"

"Because I trusted you. Figured your word was gold. Shared my innermost thoughts, fears, things that you don't share unless you're…close to the person," Dana told him.

"I have never betrayed you."

"I find that you prefer to use more sophisticated words that add a touch of polish on the B.S. that you serve."

Kent opened his mouth to continue, but Dana didn't let him "No. I'm done listening to you."

Finally, his legs moved and he walked closer to her, but she put her arms up. "I'm done having you touch me."

Despite what she had said, he pulled her into his arms. "Why?" His voice sounded hoarse.

She shuddered. "I'm done with you." She pushed away, grabbed her purse and walked out the door.

Kent felt as though he had been through a storm and emerged in a different, but oddly similar, universe. What had he done to draw that anger from her? Whatever the confusion was, he knew they could talk it through.

"Dana?" He hurried out of the room after her.

"Kent, Grace is on the line."

"For me?" He walked back into Dana's office and took the phone.

"What is going on with my granddaughter?"

"I'm trying to figure it out."

"Well, you won't have too much time to do so. Not on my dime."

"Are you firing me?"

"Consider it services rendered. Your final check will be in the mail."

Kent had never been terminated from a contract before. He'd heard about it from his fellow competitors, who had worked with difficult personalities. Nothing pleased their clients. Eventually they were fired from the job. In his mind, his competitors should have seen the termination coming and planned accordingly.

In this case, he had been totally blindsided, so much so that he couldn't figure out where to focus his energies to remedy the problem.

He walked out of the building and stared down both directions of the street. Every small act took a lot of brain power to focus and kick aside all the thoughts crowding his brain, demanding answers. He picked a direction, not caring where it took him. His feet shuffled along with a haphazard momentum and his shoulder occasionally bumped a passerby. A muffled apology and a small overhead wave were his standard responses to irritable victims.

An hour later, he sat on a park bench, looking at the athletically inclined, the young at heart, and children who didn't know how fickle the world could be. He closed his eyes and turned his face up toward the sun for its warmth. Through and through, though, he felt cold.

Rejected. Fired. Tossed onto his butt. His triumphant turn in the U.S. hadn't mustered up enough glory for its end to be epic. He had worked hard and received a boost from Grace, but the rest had been up to him. For every client she'd recommended, he had to prove that Grace wasn't his besotted mentor.

He headed back to the hotel. Time to go home. Time to take his sweetest memories from the recent events back with him, though Dana and Grace's accusations still hurt and he wanted to hit something, hard.

One message was left for him on the hotel phone. Please let it be her, he thought. Please let it be an April Fool's joke, although they were in May. He'd hang on to anything that could give him a second chance. The message played through to the end. No, Dana wouldn't be returning. No, Grace did not rescind his termination. Henry, dear gentle Henry, had said he'd be over in the next hour to talk. His voice left no doubt that he was coming to finish the job that his wife and granddaughter started.

Many had said, Don't mess with the Meadows family. They are like a nighttime drama, the Meadowses. They may fight among themselves, but to make an enemy of one Meadows is to draw the wrath of all. He wondered how many would follow him to England to continually plunge a knife in his chest. He didn't dare ask the question in their presence—if he still could—because one of them was bound to answer.

Henry was prompt. He called the hotel to announce his arrival and Kent provided him with the room number. Meeting in a restaurant or other public setting in the hotel was more suitable for Kent's purposes, but he suspected that the conversation could get intense. While the other members of the clan had come at him without warning, he wasn't going to stand idly by and be accused by Henry. One thing he wasn't was a whipping boy for the Meadows family.

"Good afternoon, Henry. Come in and have a seat," he said when the man appeared at the door

As he waited for Henry to be seated, Kent still wondered how he and Grace had gotten together and remained as close as they were all these years, despite their long marriage. "Can I get you something to drink? Water, coffee...?"

"Water."

"I'm here because the two women who are the lights of my life are unhappy. And that is an understatement. I don't have a habit of influencing their emotions so that they must only be happy. In this case, I take it personally because I reached out to you, I liked you, and you were conniving to get the better part of Meadows Media."

"I am at a loss," Kent admitted. "Accusations are flying hard at me. Character names that I'd rather never hear again after this are being painted to my skin. And I have yet to understand what I have done."

"If you say it's only business and not personal, I will pop you in that British pretty-boy mouth."

"I'm not saying anything." Kent made a big production of pouring himself a drink. Water wouldn't do in this crisis. He went for the espresso machine.

"A week ago, Dana got a call from an interested buyer for the Meadows radio station. She hadn't put it out in the industry that it was up for sale, but she wouldn't walk away from a deal."

Kent waited for the tie-in to him.

"Then she, the interested buyer, alluded to being your business…and, well, intimate partner, who seeks out companies that need to sell off assets quickly. That it was your estimation that, under Dana's management, she would be selling off chunks of Meadows Media."

"Why would I ever say something like that? And to whom?"

"Dana had the woman investigated and, sure enough, she did work with IPOs. Your name wasn't linked with them in business, at least on paper. But you certainly were linked as her partner."

"Agatha?"

"Penelope Agatha Browles. See, I had to make it my business to check on Dana's accusations."

"I had no business dealings with Agatha. Yes, we dated once, but I don't even know what she's doing now."

"Well, she's doing enough, if you ask me. The questions from the interviewer, those were the questions that Agatha had asked Dana. I don't know how she managed to get a famous business journalist in her palm, but she did."

Kent needed a moment. But Henry's quiet anger promised not to be quiet any longer.

"You had better say something…good."

"This has been so elaborate that I'm not sure that I can get you to listen."

"Pour me a touch of whatever you've got. I liked you once; maybe I can like you again."

Kent didn't know how he'd manage to clear his name. As long as Henry was willing to stay the course with him, though, he'd answer any questions.

By the time he left this room, he had one important clean sweep to make back in England. Then, he was going to do everything in his power to win back Dana.

Chapter 16

Kent didn't leave from his hotel and head over to Meadows, as he'd originally planned. He had business to take care of in England. Thankfully, Henry was back in his camp and wholeheartedly felt that he had to tie up loose ends.

Jet lag had no power over white-hot anger. Calmness eventually settled over Kent that allowed him to function as if all was well with the world. Once he arrived back in London and checked in with his office, he drove his car to Clapham.

"Hey, Kent, didn't expect to see you." Conrad did his shadow-boxing greeting, but dropped his hands at Kent's frigid lack of response.

"Did you know what Agatha was up to?"

"Agatha? Please do not mention that name to me. You should have added psycho to the list of things wrong with that woman." Conrad pointed his finger at him. "First, I thought she was ready to move on. I thought she was heading out of town on a fabulous job. That's what she wanted you to believe to get you back. I was just the simpleton to think that she was falling for me."

"Did you tell her anything about me or Dana?"

"A teensy bit."

Kent glared at Conrad.

"I was tired of her talking about you. I'd met Dana at your parents' and thought she was a fantastic woman. You love her. She loves you. It was time for Agatha to move on…with me. So, yes, I kind of rubbed it in about you and Dana."

"You fathead."

Conrad patted his face. A frown imprinted itself on his forehead, as he looked ready to protest.

"You stirred her up like a snake." Kent filled him in on the gritty details. "First, I was going to kick your everloving arse. Then I was going to go and have a showdown with Agatha, but that's probably what she's hoping for."

"Um…thank you for not pounding my face. And Agatha has to know that this wasn't going to win her any points with you."

"I don't think she cared. Or maybe she didn't think that I'd find out."

"Now what?"

"I'm bringing in the big guns. Grace Meadows."

"Dana's grandmother. The one who you said fired you?" Conrad scratched his head. "Not sure if you've gone batty, but she doesn't like you."

"Henry will take care of that better than I could. That's her husband."

Conrad shrugged, looking confused.

"This can be Grace's final throw-down. Someone

messed with her baby, in this case, babies—Meadows Media and Dana."

"I think you've become positively American on me."

"I'll leave the stiff upper lip thing to you."

"But I want to come with you," Conrad said with a whine.

"Why?"

"I think American women are smashing." Conrad pulled open his desk drawer and pulled out a mirror. "I must be a good catch. They love a brother with an accent. Look at Idris Elba. They have mad, mad love for him."

"First, I can't believe you have a mirror in your desk. Second, you don't have Idris's height or charisma."

"Doesn't matter. I just have to say, 'I like it shaken, not stirred' in my posh Brit accent and panties will be flying off."

"I'm heading over to my folks', going home to pack a few more things for a longer stay, and then I'm hitting the next plane out." Kent shook Conrad's hand and pulled him in for a hug. "Hold down the fort for me."

"Tell Dana I'm sorry."

"Sure thing."

"Ask her if she's got any sisters, cousins, maids…"

Kent left Conrad laughing and still calling out, his voice coming now from the open office window. He didn't know how long he'd be in the U.S., if he'd be an intercontinental commuter, but whatever it took, he was on his way back to get his woman.

Did CEOs call in sick? Dana was sure that they also came down with the flu and stomach viruses and Sunday blues about having to go to work on Monday.

How many had a broken heart as a diagnosis? she wondered.

She knew that bed rest, a dark bedroom, and lots of chips, chocolate and soda weren't necessarily the cure, but that they had enough powers to mask the symptoms, at least temporarily. The crying fits, well, nothing seemed to stem those.

Grace had sent Leona over to check on her. She got treated like a salesman at the door, while Dana stayed hidden behind a curtain until she gave up and left. As added protection against an invasion, since Leona had keys, Dana put on the security locks.

Dressed in a ratty T-shirt, she filled an empty plastic margarine container with her favorite cereal, poured in the milk, and grabbed a spoon. Finding a comfortable spot on the couch, she folded her feet into a lotus position and ate her cereal, staring at the switched-off TV screen.

A banging on the door interrupted her mulish contemplation about how much life sucked. Grace obviously wasn't letting up by sending Leona over for another round of being ignored. Well, Dana didn't mind playing the game, because she was sure to win.

"Dana, open this darn door. Now." It was Belinda's voice.

"For heaven's sake," Dana muttered, digging deeper into the couch. As if she'd open the door for her cousin.

"We know you're in there."

First Belinda, now Fiona.

"I can see you." A distorted face pressed against the glass patio door. "Why are you sitting there like you're a guru on a mountaintop? Come and open the door. I am a policewoman. I can break your glass."

"You'd need a reason."

"I smell smoke. Belinda, do you smell smoke?"

"I see an unconscious body."

Dana watched Fiona pick up a rock. "Don't you dare!"

she shouted. She didn't want to budge. "Piss off!" Now she was talking like she was British.

"I know you're not talking to me like that." Belinda was the biggest of the three cousins. And she was known for a heavy hand when they played tag back in the day.

Dana wanted to have her moment in peace. Why couldn't they all let her be?

"I got permission from Grace to break a window."

This was Grace's house. Grace had been sympathetic when she'd explained why her interview went south. They had bonded by chanting a mantra calling for the "death of Kent." Getting her cousins to mount an invasion felt like some sort of betrayal.

Dana slowly unwound her legs. She set down her cereal.

"Oh, hurry up. I'm getting stung by something out here in this garden with all these darn flowers." Fiona had the patience of a pea.

Dana opened the patio door and returned to her couch with the cereal bowl clutched to her stomach. "I don't want to talk."

"Good. Because we don't want to listen to your B.S." Belinda eyed her cereal bowl.

"Why are you coming at me like I'm the bad guy?" Dana filled her mouth with cereal.

"Oh, honey, we are here because you need us." Fiona came over and hugged her.

"Since when?" Dana didn't feel like any hugs.

"Is this your first heartbreak?" Trust Belinda to be blunt.

Dana nodded.

"The first is always tough." Fiona patted Dana's hand. Fiona's phone buzzed, but she ignored it.

Belinda continued, "Look, the key to getting better is not letting the world know how much it hurts."

"Oh, that's really nice. You want her to pretend she doesn't feel like crap because her boyfriend still had his hook-up while he was with her."

"That sounds as ugly as it feels." Dana looked at the rest of her cereal, now soggy and disgusting. "Did Grace tell you to come and harass me?"

"No. Grandpa did." Fiona was rapidly texting.

"What?"

"He said that he was taking over this time." Belinda looked at Fiona for confirmation.

Fiona nodded. "Taking over from Grandma. She was all worked up about something. The two of them are pretty funny, now that Grandma is home all the time. I think he's wishing that she had something to do."

"At least they have each other. Here's to long-lasting love." Belinda had retrieved the cereal box in the kitchen and now ate the dry, fruity circles.

"Shut up, Belinda." Fiona motioned toward Dana as if she couldn't see her.

"I don't want your pity."

"What do you want, boo?" That was Belinda between bites.

"Call me 'boo' and I'll punch you in the nose." Her cousins had teased her mercilessly as a kid. Her crying earned her that nickname until she did punch Belinda in the nose.

"You need to freshen up. Seriously." Fiona swiped back the curtains, letting in as much sunlight as possible.

"Why? When you leave, I'll go back to what I was doing." Dana hoped they got the hint.

"You want to be looking pretty. Trust me." Belinda emptied another handful of cereal, and a few pieces went rolling under the couch. "Oops."

Something in their demeanor caught her senses, putting her on alert. "What's going on? Please tell me you're not dragging me out to a restaurant so you can shower me with your advice. Advice, may I add, that you don't even live by."

"Ouch. You're a mean thing when you're down." Fiona's phone buzzed again.

"Maybe I can help clear up some matters."

That voice was like warm caramel syrup. Dana stood, upending the cereal bowl and its contents. Her cousins hadn't moved. Instead, their grins were wide and smug.

"This was a setup." Dana gathered her wits. She had to temper her excitement at seeing Kent. She had to remember that he was the enemy.

"Call it an intervention," Fiona said.

"I couldn't wait in the car any longer," Kent interjected.

"She was being a bit stubborn, our wee lass," Belinda attempted to say while chewing.

"Um…that's Scottish. Kent is British." Dana rolled her eyes at her cousin's mockery.

"I'm not sure that was even Scottish." Kent winked at Dana.

Her belly flipped and then flopped.

"Ladies, thank you for getting her to open the door. Please tell Grace that I'll stop by when I'm done."

Her cousins hugged her in turn and wished him luck.

"Looks like you've won over the family. Did you cast a spell? Did you offer up your firstborn? Did you slide a check to Grace's favorite charity? Or did you do the usual B.S. flattery that renders one incapable of using their brain?"

"Actually, all of the above, especially the one about casting a spell," Kent fired back.

"You have no right to be snippy." She walked into the kitchen to get products to clean up the floor. By the time she'd returned, he was on his hands and knees, scooping the circular cereal bits back into the bowl. "I can manage. Been doing so all my life." She pushed him out of the way to put down the paper towels.

"Would you agree that we have something of a perfect storm here?"

"It's definitely a storm. I'm not sure how perfect it is."

"Well, there are several factors coming from various directions and all meeting at the same time. So what, in a singular event, would be a minor skirmish has now turned into a colossal conflict."

"Get to the point." She gathered up the wasted contents of her cereal bowl and headed into the kitchen. She didn't want to hear about any weather-related analogies.

"You had the misfortune of indirectly meeting my ex-girlfriend, Agatha Browles. I was the target of her wrath until she learned about you from Conrad. Agatha made destroying what we had her focus. She picked at your fears and pushed at them with scenarios that sounded real." He paused. "None of it was real. None."

"You didn't talk to her about me?"

He shook his head.

"It sounded like what you'd say."

"I'm sure it did. But that was your mind playing tricks. That's the other point. You were already wondering if you should stay with me. You somehow felt that you didn't deserve to be happy. Total contentment with a career and a personal life. You've used others as your measuring stick and feel that you don't deserve having it all."

"Career and personal lives are two demanding masters. Working on one without the other feels like a monumental betrayal. I'm ready to dedicate my life to one."

"I hope that you didn't see it as an either-or, but, if you do go down that path, I want to be the one that you follow."

"You'd want me to walk away from Meadows Media?"

"No, I don't want you to walk away from the career that needs you. But I'm not going to stand on a lie and act like I wouldn't be devastated if you picked your career over me. I'd fight dirty if I had to in order to get you back in my life. We are a team, Dana, you and me. The problem is that you continue to see only you in your world. I'm not sure where in all those swirling thoughts you have me."

Dana excused herself to change into something less intimate, less revealing. Besides, she needed a bit of physical distance to bolster her weakening resolve. When she returned, Kent was still standing in the kitchen. She hoisted herself onto the kitchen counter. Wherever he was in her thoughts, she knew where he was at this very minute. He was pleading his case. She didn't seem to be putting up much of a fight. Agatha sounded real—kooky, but real.

Once the common enemy was removed, there was still more to be dealt with.

"You are a fixer. It's how you make your living." She was very conscious that she was wearing a T-shirt. Her hair was unkempt and crying out for conditioner. Her emotions were a bit fragile. But she was ready to be CEO nonetheless. What he'd accomplished in getting her ready for the position was phenomenal. "You see me as a product, a brand that moves between either the right or wrong decision, without a thought toward my hang-ups and nuances with regard to the way I think. I feel like a prizefighter being conditioned for the fight of her life, and also a statistic in your belt."

Kent bowed his head.

The doorbell sounded. This time, Dana swore. Who was left to barge in to fix her life? She stormed to the door and flung it open. "Grandpa? What are you doing here? Is Grace okay?" Dana stepped onto the porch to see if there was an ambulance on the property.

"No, dear, it's only me." He walked in past her and stopped short when he saw Kent. His face broke into a wide grin. "Oh, good, I'm so glad you two made up. I was afraid that I'd missed Kent and I wanted to offer my congratulations."

Kent said nothing. His downward gaze said it all.

Dana came in behind her grandfather and motioned for him to have a seat "Oh, this doesn't feel good." Henry looked between them. "I'd hoped that you could work out the issues. You've got something—"

"Please don't say 'special.' That's too cliché for what's happening here. I was explaining to Kent why I am choosing to stick with Meadows Media as the only master to serve in my life. I plan to fly solo with my career aspirations. It's best to sever the emotional ties. And he can go do his job without dealing with the personal investment of my success or failure weighing on his résumé."

"Kent, are you going to let her get away with that ratty logic? These Meadows women will run all over you if you show any signs of weakness. I didn't realize that this one had learned it so young."

"Grandpa, I'm not in the mood."

"Not in the mood for good sense, if you ask me," Kent spoke up.

"Ah, the wolf has finally awakened." Henry clapped his hands. He shifted his gaze to Kent as if waiting for his verbal parry to Dana.

"You can't run Meadows Media without me."

"I don't need you to help me run my grandmother's company."

"No, you don't. You have a qualified executive staff and loads of loyal employees for that. But you only think of one aspect of running that company. You only think about the physical demands and at your age, yes, you've got the stamina. But there are other necessary components that you don't have on your own. Not unless you're super-natural or a robot."

"Grace did it."

"Grace didn't do it. I know you've put her on a pedestal. But take off the blinders. Look at your grandfather. He was, and is, as much a contributing factor to Meadows Media's success as your grandmother. I didn't realize it until I saw how my mother and stepfather had a rhythm that worked for them and brought them happiness in each of their individual pursuits—she as a homemaker and he as a mechanic. Simple lives built by something so complicated and beautiful."

Dana sat next to Henry. Her dear, quiet grandfather who had observed the lives of his children and grandchildren. Who had been taken for granted by all, but had the patience and wisdom of a sage when any one of them bothered to bring their problems to him.

Kent's profound declaration was like the removal of a veil from her eyes. Understanding dawned like light that grew brighter as the shade was removed.

"I want to be there with you, at your side, even behind you cheering you on. I'm not afraid of your light and I'm not afraid of your shadow. Maybe I am overzealous. I see life as a competition. I do think in terms of knockouts. But my love for you and who you are isn't about a win, lose or draw. It's about building and holding on to each other for the long term. It's about filling in with our strengths and weaknesses, forming a union that is unbreakable, that no one can rip apart, even when they spread salacious lies that would normally rock a foundation."

"Grandpa?"

"Yes, sweetheart."

"Is he really good folk?"

"He's the real thing." Henry pushed himself up. "Can I now say congratulations? Grace is out for another hour and I want to go light up for a quick one."

Dana nodded. She hugged her grandfather. Her tears and laughter mixed as he urged her to let him go so he could get going.

Kent hugged him, too. They didn't look like father and son, but clearly had bonded like family. "I'll be right over, so I can put out that cigar."

Henry waved and he walked briskly back to the main house.

Dana locked the door, sliding on the security chain. Then she went around the house, closing any gaps in the curtain.

"And we are under house quarantine because…?" Kent asked.

"Because, I want no more interruptions while I properly make up with my executive coach."

"I've been fired."

"Good. I have another position…or two…or three that needs to be filled."

"I hope that I'm up for the task."

She rubbed the front of his pants. "I'd say that you more than meet the qualifications."

"You only want me for my body."

"Is that all you're prepared to give me?"

"My soul."

"Hmmm."

"My heart."

"Now, you're talking. In return, I give you my heart and soul."

"What about your body?"

"It's yours forever."

Kent lowered his mouth to Dana's and sealed it with a long, searing kiss.

* * * * *

REQUEST YOUR FREE BOOKS!

2 FREE NOVELS PLUS 2 FREE GIFTS!

KIMANI ROMANCE™

Love's ultimate destination!

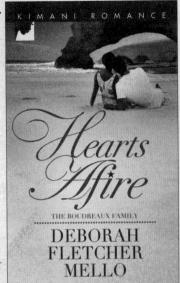

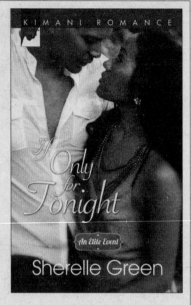

Two full-length novels featuring the dynamic and
mesmerizing Westmoreland family…

**FROM *NEW YORK TIMES* AND
USA TODAY BESTSELLING AUTHOR**

BRENDA JACKSON
WISHES FOR TOMORROW

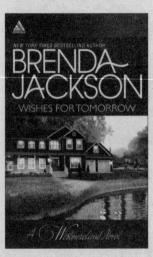

In *Westmoreland's Way*,
Dillon Westmoreland and
Pamela Novak discover mind-
blowing passion together. And
once a Westmoreland claims
the woman he wants, he won't
let anything tear them apart!

In *Hot Westmoreland Nights*,
Ramsey Westmoreland knows
better than to lust after the
hired help…but new cook
Chloe Burton proves delectably
irresistible!

"Sexy and sizzling…"
—*Library Journal* on *INTIMATE SEDUCTION*

Available now wherever books are sold!

HARLEQUIN®
www.Harlequin.com

KPBJI490114R